Day Zero

The Zero Trilogy

Book #1

A Short Collapse Series Companion Adventure

Summer Lane

Copyright 2014

WB Publishing

All Rights Reserved

No part of this book may be reproduced in any form, except to quote in reviews or interviews, without the express permission of the author. Any unauthorized distribution of this body of work is illegal and punishable by law.

This is a work of fiction. Any parallel to persons alive or dead is purely coincidental and is not intended by the author.

For you, readers.

Thank you for everything.

Prologue

Hollywood was dark. That was the first thing Elle noticed when she stood on the ridgeline, just behind the Hollywood sign. She had never seen it like this before. The city had always been brimming with life, with activity. Even after Day Zero, when the lights went out, there were fires and riots. Noise.

Now there was nothing.

Elle pulled her jacket tighter, trying to stop herself from shuddering. If the stories were true...if Uncle was right...then there would be nothing left for Elle here. The silence was telling – no noise meant no people.

Of course, she couldn't be entirely sure.

There might be people somewhere.

She started climbing down the ridgeline, onto the dirt trail. The hill was dry. Dead grass snapped under her shoes. She had never felt so alone or cold in her life.

Later, as she hit the streets of Hollywood, the utter silence overwhelmed her. It was thick, like a curtain. The darkness, the quietness. The deadness. She knew she had made a mistake coming back here. She needed to go back to the ranch, back to Aunt and Uncle. They would understand why she left, and they would welcome her home.

She didn't get the chance.

A man came around the corner, thickset and heavily tattooed.

Elle stared at him.

She shouldn't have come back.

Chapter One

West Hollywood, California

Elle sat cross-legged on the edge of the roof, watching the empty street. She'd been up here for a while. This was the first time in a week it had stopped raining long enough to sit outside.

She brushed her black hair out of her blue eyes. The bank across the street was quiet. So was the bus stop, the pizza restaurant next door and the clothing shop catty corner to the streetlights. Elle swung her legs over the top of the roof, climbing back down to the street. She rounded the front of the building and peeked through the broken windows. The menu above the counter said *Millions of Milkshakes* in bright letters. It had been a prominent place, once. A milkshake bar known for hosting celebrities and athletes in the heart of the most famous city on earth.

Everything had changed since the electromagnetic pulse.

Planes had fallen from the sky and technology had failed, leaving Hollywood and all of its glamour in the dark. The power was out for good. The world was a different place.

The world was dangerous.

The front counter was dusty. Most of the restaurant was dirty and looted. Elle wondered if there was any food left. An ice cream parlor wouldn't be the first place people would look for food. After all, ice cream melts.

She checked over her shoulder and slid a small knife from her shoe. She angled her thin, short frame under the slivers of broken window glass and slipped inside, feet crunching against plastic wrappers and dirt.

She didn't like being this exposed.

The building was cold. It smelled fetid. Something was rotting. A dead animal? Putrid food? She didn't really want to know.

Elle walked behind the counter. The back of the kitchen was dark. Elle wasn't crazy about searching it, but she pressed ahead anyway, the possibility of finding something to eat overcoming her anxiety.

She slid into the kitchen, squinting to make out the shape of the counter and the fridges. There was just enough light coming in from the front windows to see the cupboards. She yanked them open. There were several containers of sprinkles inside, a package of paper cups and a stack of napkins. Elle sighed, disappointed, and removed her backpack from her shoulders. She stuffed the cups and napkins inside. She could use them later.

She searched the other cupboards. There was an expired bottle of chocolate sauce, a box of toothpicks and a sealed box of sour candy. Elle tossed the candy and toothpicks into her backpack, searched the place one more time, and zipped it back up.

Her heart sank. She was hungry, and a box of candy wasn't going to fill her empty stomach. She strapped the backpack on again and headed toward the front of the building, pausing at the window, scanning the street.

There. At the east end of the boulevard. Someone was watching. A man.

She dropped into a crouch, heart pounding against her ribcage.

Elle didn't dare move. She knew how this game worked. The *American Apparel* building next to the crosswalk was where she had seen the flicker of movement.

She kept looking, searching. There it was again.

A black flash, a tiny streak. Another one by the bus stop. Two people? Three?

Great. I'm surrounded.

She looked up and down the street. Counted the dead cars sitting at the curb, estimating the amount of cover she would have on her way from Point A to Point B. It would be close, but she could do it if she moved fast.

And she was good at that.

She focused on her breathing as the adrenaline surged. She could hear the blood rushing in her ears. This was a bad situation. *They* were always out there, looking for victims.

She shuddered and refocused her mind.

Stay focused. Don't let them trap you!

Elle checked the back door in the building, but it was locked tight, rusted shut. She returned to the front, kneeling near the broken windows. She leaned forward on her fingers, like a runner preparing for a sprint. She ran fast and smooth on the wet sidewalk, straining to keep her footsteps silent. She huddled behind the first car that was parked on the curb, breathing hard.

Elle dared a glance behind her. Nobody. Yet.

She ran again, to the next car. Cover to cover. *They* could be anywhere, and staying behind something big was the only way to make sure that she would be safe. She made it all the way down the block.

I'm almost there.

She stopped behind the last car on the block, her fingers pressed against the cold asphalt. Someone jumped onto the hood of the car, making a heavy thud. Elle jerked backward and stood, holding her arms up defensively.

He was tall, dressed in black. Snakelike dreadlocks hung down his back. His dark eyes looked dead. He was holding a sword, a Japanese Katana. He leaped forward and charged at Elle.

Elle didn't scream. She reached inside her jacket and drew her handgun. The words *Smith and Wesson* were engraved on the side of the barrel. Elle pointed the weapon at the center of his chest and fired. The shot was piercing. It echoed down the street, shattering the unearthly silence of the city. He jerked backward, hitting the car. He landed on his knees, staring at Elle as blood seeped through the material of his shirt. She stepped forward and kicked him in the chest, knocking him flat on his back. Elle never took her eyes from his as the life left his body. A red ribbon of blood streamed from the side of his mouth, his eyes fixed on the sky.

Elle scanned the area. She saw no other threats, so she holstered the handgun and stepped forward, kneeling next to his body. She searched his jacket and pants, finding a handful of bullets and a package of gum. She took the goods and picked up the sword, testing its weight in her hands. She took the scabbard and stood, overlooking the street.

The gunshot had sent others into hiding. Other people – more dangerous ones – would regroup and emerge again. It was time to get moving.

All was silent once again.

The city had been a warzone for ten months. After the collapse – after the world ended – *they* came: Omega. The shadow army. The invasion force. They were everywhere and nowhere all at once. An eye in the sky. A patrol on the street. Where did they come from? Nobody knew. What did they want? Us.

They wanted *all* of us.

They used chemical weapons against us. They destroyed millions of the civilian population of Los Angeles. Omega moved their center of operations to the Port of Los Angeles and downtown L.A., leaving Hollywood and Santa Monica mostly abandoned.

Those places belonged to the dead now.

Well. The dead and people like Elle: foragers and survivors.

The rest of the state was squashed under the Omega invasion. Concentration camps corralled citizens into forced slave labor. Omega ruled with an iron fist, and anyone who dared challenge them died.

But not all hope was lost. Grassroots militia groups sprung up in the areas controlled by Omega, and the people resisted the takeover. In the Central Valley, Omega had been pushed back, had suffered heavy casualties.

Few civilians remained in Los Angeles after the chemical attacks. Those that did were usually looking for food, medical supplies or lost family members. The chances of finding either of those things were slim to none. Yet some people returned, and many formed the street gangs of Los Angeles. It was a place dictated by the brutality of an invading army and the savagery of desperate survivors.

It was a deadly game; the survival of the fittest. Only the smartest – or the most ruthless – survived. The rest fell by the wayside, either starving to death or falling prey to Omega or the street gangs. Those who managed to avoid death by starvation or murder clung to the hope that order and peace would somehow be restored.

There was no more order, no more security. No more civility between average citizens. It was kill or be killed. Common trust was gone. The rules had changed.

No one knew that better than Elle.

When the electromagnetic pulse hit Los Angeles, she had been fourteen years old, a student at Beverly Hills High School, and the daughter of wealthy Hollywood socialites. Raised in a house where strict discipline and work ethic were encouraged, she pursued her passion of martial arts and gymnastics. Elle, her parents, and her brother lived in an apartment in Westwood, just a few miles from Hollywood Boulevard.

Her first semester as a freshman at Beverly Hills High School came to an abrupt end when the electromagnetic pulse hit. Her world changed in an instant.

Everything fell apart.

Elle turned and ran. Her best defense was her speed and agility. The sun was setting, and she knew what that meant. Before long, street predators would be roving the city. She needed to get back to her hiding place.

The shot that she had just fired still rang in her head. She hated having to defend herself from people like that, from desperate, starving killers. Elle's guess was that the man she had killed had been a member of the Klan, the city's most organized gang. They were powerful.

They were deadly.

Santa Monica itself was a beautiful city, once. The apartment complexes rose like sharp bits of broken teeth into the sky. Vegetation wound its way through apartment balconies and around dead car frames. Elle kept running, breathing hard, sweat running down her forehead, the back of her neck. She had blood on her cheek – she'd caught a spray of it when she had shot the gang member at *Millions of Milkshakes.*

She hooked a left and dropped prone behind an overturned trashcan. She could smell the ocean, fresh and salty and cold. Across the street, there was a beautiful, unattended park, wet with rain. It looked like nature was taking over, taking back everything it had owned before the rise of modern civilization. And beyond that, Highway 1 – The Pacific Coast Highway – paralleled the beach below the cliff. The shoreline extended as far as the eye could see, dotted with empty beach houses. In fact, you could even see the blackened remains of the cliff-side mansions of Malibu if you looked hard enough.

But Elle had already seen all that.

To her back was a white apartment building, long ago abandoned by the residents before the chemical weapons. A stairway led to the front entrance. Elle checked left, checked right. She stood and sprinted up the stairs, pushing the door open. She slammed it shut behind her, lowering the lock – a heavy piece of wood, serving both as a crossbar and an intruder alarm. It was dark inside.

This was her safe zone, her hideaway.

She felt her way up a dark hallway, trotting up steps. She could barely see anything besides the general shape of the railing and the steps. She reached the fourth floor and counted her steps.

Seven, eight, nine, ten...here we are.

She felt for the door handle. There it was, just like she had practiced. She turned the handle and the door opened. A slit of late sunlight fell across her face. She stepped inside and closed the door, locked it. She breathed a sigh of relief.

Safe. For now.

The apartment was a modern loft. One bedroom, one bathroom, and a kitchen. Whoever lived here had been some kind of a poet. Poetry books were everywhere – along with CDs and DVDs of poetry reading. Some of it was weird, some of it was pretty. Elle was never into poetry, but reading it sometimes helped to pass the long, lonely hours of the day.

She hated those hours.

She dropped her backpack on the carpet and walked to the window. She pulled back the curtain enough so that she could watch the street below. She was on the corner, so she could see Santa Monica Boulevard and Ocean Boulevard at the same time.

Her only blind spot was the alley behind the apartment building, but she had no way to get a good view of that. She'd been living here for three weeks, and so far she hadn't had any trouble. She hoped it stayed that way.

From her spot at the window, Elle could see the Santa Monica Pier. The brightly colored rollercoaster wound around the Ferris wheel. It looked lonely. Empty. It had been a long time since the pier had glowed with lights and echoed with the laughter of fun-seeking crowds.

Tomorrow, she would visit the pier.

Chapter Two

Elle had been looking at the Santa Monica Pier for nine months. Every evening, every day. She would look for any sign of movement, of habitation. But there was never anything, other than the occasional nomadic fisherman. It made Elle curious. It made her brave.

It made her stupid, too, sometimes. Reckless.

She sat on the floor of the apartment, legs propped up on the couch, head on the floor. The window was open just a crack, enough to let the cool sea breeze inside the stuffy room. Elle closed her eyes and pretended that she was home, watching television while she waited for her mom to come back from the grocery store.

She sat up abruptly.

Mom was never coming back from the grocery store.

Elle was alone.

She rolled to her knees and stood up, walking into the kitchen. She didn't have a lot of supplies here. A few canned goods – carrots, peas and creamed corn – and two tins of tuna. Elle hated tuna, but she'd eat it anyway if it were all she had. She'd eaten worse in the last year. A lot worse.

The sour candy that she'd found at *Millions of Milkshakes* hadn't filled the hole in her stomach. Sooner or later she'd have to face reality: Santa Monica and Hollywood was running out of food. She was going to have to move on.

It'd probably be better that way, she told herself. *Right...?*

No. Omega was everywhere. Nowhere was safe.

But she didn't want to leave. She knew these streets, and it was the only thing in her life that was familiar. She had grown up here. She had visited the theater with her father, eaten lunch on Saturday afternoons with her mother at the beach and built sandcastles with her brother. This was her home.

If she left, she would be a nomad. A wanderer.

No one really knew what was beyond the city.

Elle put the cans back on the counter, ignoring her growling stomach. The food was a precious commodity. Flavorful stuff like carrots or green beans was becoming less available. Elle had become a skilled forager, but even she could barely find enough to eat anymore.

She organized her backpack again. She kept it filled with essential supplies: water, food, matches, bandages, iodine, maps, a knife and ammunition for her 1911 Smith and Wesson handgun. They were necessary items, important for survival.

Several times during the night she heard noises coming from somewhere inside the apartment building. Creaks, groans and thumping sounds. She would freeze with every sound, terrified that she would hear a footstep. But no. For the most part, the noises were just from loose boards or windows moving in the September breeze.

Birds had started returning to Los Angeles a few months ago. The chemical weapons – whatever they were, no one could be sure – had wiped out all forms of life. Dogs, cats, birds and bugs. Elle often wondered if a low level of poison was still seeping out of the walls of every building in the city, slowing killing her. It was a terrifying thought, but she didn't care as much as she should.

If she died, she died.

Nobody was going to miss her. There was nobody left.

Elle finished restocking her backpack. She kept her pack with her at all times, always filled with a little bit of food and medicine. The possibility that she might not make it back to the apartment at the end of the day was very real. She'd found that out months ago, shivering and starving for three days in the basement of a sushi house, waiting for Klan gang members to move on. She'd wished that she'd had food in her pack then.

She wouldn't make the same mistake twice.

As a general rule, Elle wouldn't eat anything in the city that wasn't sealed in an airtight container like a plastic bag or a can. She didn't know what kinds of chemical weapons had been released on the city, but it would be stupid to eat food that might be soaked in the stuff. She'd seen seagulls fly in off the coastline, eat garbage from the overflowing trash containers, and drop dead.

She was living in a biological waste zone, and she knew it.

Yeah, I should definitely move on, she thought. *But what if what's out there is worse than what's in Los Angeles?*

The fear of the unknown is what kept Elle in the city.

Omega had power. So much power that they had destroyed the technological infrastructure of the most powerful nation on earth. For all Elle knew, they might have taken over the entire world by now.

There might not *be* a safe place anymore.

Chapter Three

Zero.

There it was, spray-painted across the first board on the Santa Monica Pier. Elle stared at it, swallowing a nervous lump in her throat. The pier was creaking in the wind. Every time a wave hit the support beams below, the boardwalk shuddered in the early morning light. It was foggy, wet and cold.

Elle hauled a fishing pole over her shoulder, one of the most valuable items she had foraged from the city. She had bait in her backpack, a can full of worms she had dug up from the muddy soil in the park above the beach. Coming to the pier to fish was something she had been trying to work up the courage to do for a long time. She'd heard that people used to fish from the pier in the past. Elle was starving, and she would do anything for food.

Zero.

It had been painted across the railings, on the back of buildings, on cars parked in the parking lot next to the pier. Elle knew what it meant. It meant the world was over. The *modern* world, anyway. It meant *back to the drawing board.*

The boardwalk stretched far into the water. Abandoned amusement attractions paralleled the pier – a merry-go-round, a bicycle shop. The once-famous Muscle Beach stretched out on the left, below the pier.

Elle remembered seeing this place at night as a little girl. Before the Collapse. It was lit up like a Christmas tree, rainbow colored and glowing.

She started walking. She was aware of how exposed she was. Anybody could be watching her. *Anybody.*

Her hunger drove her onward.

She kept walking down the boardwalk, moving from cover to cover, staying in the shadows, watching for danger. The sound of the waves and seagulls on the railing were the only things she could hear. It was so silent. So sad. She continued, reaching a sign that said *Pacific Park*.

The letters stretched across the entrance, colorful but faded. Elle stood and looked at it. A rollercoaster and other amusement rides were clustered around the pier. Elle walked under the lettered archway. Every building here was a faded neon color. Green, blue, red, and yellow. It was cheery, but in this atmosphere, little more than a sick joke.

Nothing was fun anymore. Even this was just an empty husk.

There was a rollercoaster, an elevator launch, an octopus spin, a Ferris wheel. There were kiddie rides and carnival games. She searched the rest of the park, pawing through a restaurant called *The Harbor Grill*. There was nothing edible left. It had been too long. Anything here had either been looted or exposed to the poison of the chemical weapons. There was no food.

Elle sat near the railing at the end of the pier, beyond the attractions, near an empty souvenir shop. She checked her line, baited and weighted the hook, and casted it into the water below. She had brought a plastic bag in her backpack, in case she caught a fish. She stared at the water below as she sat, cross-legged, trying to keep her mind off the pain in her stomach.

She was just so *hungry*.

Elle thought about Los Angeles, and how impossible it was to find food anymore. But leaving the city frightened Elle. What if the world outside Los Angeles was worse? What if Omega had really destroyed everything?

She shuddered.

I've got to make a decision.

And that's when she heard it.

Human voices.

Elle slid into the shadows. She hid beneath a plastic picnic table and looked up the pier, back toward the mainland. There were *people*. Several of them. At least eight – maybe more. She couldn't tell from here.

Elle's chest constricted.

Someone *had* seen her. Klan members, by the looks of it. Had to be. Omega didn't come to the beach unless they had a very good reason.

Elle slowly crawled backward. She knew the Klan well, better than most.

The Klan members were sauntering up the pier, making no attempt to hide their presence. They knew that Elle had nowhere to run. She gritted her teeth.

I never should have come out here.

Now she would be *forced* out of the city. Or worse, killed.

She turned and sprinted to the back of *Pacific Park.* Nowhere to hide, nowhere to run. She looked at her fishing pole, wedged between the railing, the line moving in the waves.

She flinched as she turned her back on the fishing pole – such a valuable item.

Don't think about that now.

The buildings were small and packed together. The Klan members would spread out and pin her down. She couldn't hide here. Not for very long, anyway. She ran to the railing, peeked over the edge. The waves were deep and unforgiving.

She licked the salty spray of the sea off her lips and swung her legs over the side. "Please, God," she whispered. "Let me survive this."

She lowered herself below the boards of the pier, hanging by her hands. Her legs dangled over the water – a long drop if she fell. Mazes of wooden support beams crisscrossed beneath the pier like stiff webbing. Elle curled her fingers around the first one parallel to the underside of the pier. She swung her body back and forth, gaining enough momentum to latch the heel of her shoe onto a beam. Now she was balancing horizontally between two beams. She moved one hand forward, then the other. She pushed herself up and sat on top of the first beam.

It's not so different from gymnastics class, she told herself.

She pulled her legs under her and crouched like a cat, studying the maze of wooden poles under the pier. They stretched from here to the shore. She could very, *very* carefully crawl back...if the Klan didn't figure out where she was by then.

She moved with caution, slipping from beam to beam. The crash and bubble of the tide swirling below the boardwalk drowned out the sound of her movements.

The pier shuddered slightly and Elle stopped. She held her breath. They were walking right above her head. They were shouting, but she couldn't make out their words. What were they saying? Probably something about killing Elle. That was the Klan way, after all.

Their boots made the pier shake, and Elle found herself sweating. But they couldn't see her down here.

Come on, keep going. You're almost there.

Almost being a relative term.

The pier was over a thousand feet long – and that didn't count the boardwalk bridge. Elle had to crawl almost a fourth of a mile to get back to the mainland. And once she did, she would have to run.

She focused her mind on moving from one beam to another. Since the Collapse, she had learned to be patient. To think ahead, but to live in the moment. Panicking in a time of crisis didn't do any good. She'd seen that.

Staying calm was what had saved her from the Klan in the past.

Focus, focus!

Hours seemed to pass. She stretched from beam to beam, until her hands were blistered from gripping the wood. Splinters bit into her palms. She was only thirty or so yards away from the beach. Once she reached the mainland, she would be able to drop onto the beach. And *then* she would run. She climbed, and as the pier jutted into the beach, she got about ten feet above the sand. Elle dropped. The tide swirled around her worn tennis shoes, cold and crisp.

She peeked around the corner, above her head. No sign of the enemy. If she stayed left, behind the shelter of the buildings on the pier, she might be able to avoid being seen.

She kept her head down and crawled along the side of the pier, out of sight. It was slow going. When she finally got even with the pier, she got down on her knees and crawled.

Think like a turtle, she told herself, smiling wryly. *Slow and steady wins the race...*

That's what her mother used to tell her, anyway.

My dead mother.

She didn't stop crawling until she reached the parking lot of the *Bubba Gump Shrimp Co.* Then she stood up and sprinted to the back of the building, breathing hard. She snuck a glance at the pier. She could see the Klan members, small specks in the distance at the end of the pier. They couldn't see *her*. But she could tell by the way they were spread out around *Pacific Park* that they were searching for her.

She turned. And she ran. She did *not* want to be around when they came back this way. Her legs and lungs were strong as she put distance between herself and the enemy. She passed *SM Pier Seafood* and the *Santa Monica Pier Aquarium*, with its white paint and domed ceiling. She passed the massive parking lot on the left, full of dead cars and dead bodies. If you caught the wind, it carried the scent of the cadavers up the street.

The last collection of buildings on the strip was the dully-colored pastel restaurants and seaside souvenir shops. Vines and bushes had covered the exteriors of most of the buildings, but Elle could see that it had once been cute. A little rundown, perhaps, but because it was Santa Monica, it had probably been very pricey.

Whatever. Money didn't matter anymore. Nothing did.

Elle didn't look over her shoulder to see if the Klan members were coming back down the pier. She didn't want to scare herself, and besides – there could be danger right in front of her face. The Klan had hundreds of members – if not thousands – that dominated the streets of Los Angeles and the surrounding urban areas.

Elle paused at a street called *Moomat Ahiko Way*. It curved left and paralleled the freeway. She stopped dead in her tracks. Following this road would take her all the way back to *Ocean Avenue*, back to her little apartment, back to what she was familiar with.

But if she turned left, she would be on her way out of the city for good.

Turning left would take her to *Highway One,* the *Pacific Coast Highway.* She had stared at the freeway from her apartment window for weeks, wondering when she'd be forced to leave.

In front of her, the city loomed dark and ominous. Huge. The distant rattle and boom of gunfire echoed off the empty buildings. Elle shuddered. The fights between the street gangs and Omega were escalating with each passing day.

The cold breeze ruffled Elle's short hair. She looked behind her.

The Klan members on the pier were moving toward the beach. They had seen her, and they were running at a brisk jog. Elle wasn't worried – she could outlast them in the end. She was light and she could run many miles before she needed to stop and rest.

Left? Straight? Do I stay or do I go?

Elle closed her eyes.

And she headed back into the city.

She wasn't ready to leave yet.

Elle didn't dare go home. If the Klan saw where she lived, she'd have to find a new place to hide. It always took time and patience to find a safe zone. Somewhere she could hunker down and relax without wondering if someone was going to slit her throat while she slept.

She kept moving, checking to see if the Klan remnants from the pier were still pursuing her. They were. At least for now. She would throw them off her trail. Elle knew Hollywood and Santa Monica better than anyone. Every street, every shop, every alleyway.

She worked her way onto Ocean Boulevard and hung a left, bypassing her apartment building. She ran up the street, diving right, into a small alley that led to the back of another apartment complex. This one had been very upscale. A wrought iron fence surrounded the parking lot. Elle jammed her boots into the small spaces between the vertical bars and swung her body over the top, landing with a soft thud on the other side.

She sloshed through puddles and hurried to the back of the building, behind rows of parked cars. A lonely wind swept through the alley, and she could hear the voices of the Klan members on the boulevard. They weren't trying to be stealthy. Not at all. They wanted her to know they were coming.

To them, fear was part of the fun. It was part of the hunt.

She opened the back door and stepped inside. This was the rear entrance, and she had been here a few times before. It was her little secret. Her passageway for a quick escape.

The hallway was long and dark. It smelled of dust and…something else. She had been wandering the city long enough to differentiate between the scents of rotting food and rotting bodies. She shuddered and ran through the hall, locating the stairwell. She climbed to the top level and opened the door that led to the roof. A five-foot space between this building and the next stretched before her. Elle ran and jumped, easily clearing the distance. Yet another skill she could thank martial arts and gymnastics for.

It was a good thing she'd had hobbies before Day Zero.

She ran to the other side of the roof. A telephone pole sat about two feet away from the corner of the building. Elle hopped onto the metal pegs and climbed down, moving fast. She reached the alley.

"Gotcha!"

Elle choked on a scream. A Klan member was waiting in the shadows, armed with a wicked-looking knife. She ducked under the vicious slash of the weapon as it sliced through the air. Her attacker was an older man, sparse gray hair hanging in greasy strands to his shoulders.

She dodged him like a cat and sprinted down the alley. The heavy thud of his footsteps echoed off the buildings as she ran.

"She's down here!" the man yelled. "Over here! Come on!"

Elle didn't dare look back. She was too busy concentrating on running. She skidded around the corner. This boulevard was a little smaller than the last one. Where was she? She recited the street names in her head. She was nearing *Holly's Books*, an abandoned bookstore.

She saw it, the small shop wedged into the bottom of a hotel. She knew exactly where she was now.

Something whizzed by her left shoulder. She swerved and jerked her head left, straining to see behind her. The old man was chucking broken chunks of concrete at her, a last ditch effort to slow her escape.

Stupid, Elle thought.

But he was yelling, making an ungodly amount of noise. She needed to hide before every Klan member on this side of the city came running. Elle came to a corner and turned left, but there were people coming up the street. She went right, and there were more.

They're boxing me in, she thought, scared. *What do I do? Where do I go?*

A tiny walkway cut between a hotel and a steakhouse. Both buildings were surrounded with tall weeds. She darted into the small path. It was barely wide enough for one person.

Elle reached the end of the walkway. It stopped inside a courtyard. The shrubbery was out of control, growing through the cracks in the cement and winding around drainpipes.

She was trapped. The courtyard only had one entrance – and one exit. Her heart slammed against her ribcage. She was going to die this time. The Klan would grab her, drag her into the street, and slit her throat on the asphalt. They'd leave her dead body there as a warning to other foragers...

"Hey! Psst! Girl!"

Elle spun around, searching for the source of the voice. A window was open above her head, one of the many windows overlooking the courtyard. She stared. She saw a flash of blue eyes, frizzy blonde hair and a smattering of freckles. It was a girl, and she wasn't much older than Elle.

"Come on!" she hissed. "Climb!!"

She pointed to the drainpipe crawling up the wall. Elle didn't hesitate.

Her life was on the line, and this was a way out.

She climbed the drainpipe, pulling herself up. Her muscles strained, but Elle was nimble and quick, and she reached the open window in no time. The girl slammed the window shut. Elle sprang to her feet, panting.

"Follow me," the girl whispered.

Elle looked around. The room in which they were standing was abandoned. It had been ransacked. The girl ran and Elle followed. She was taller than Elle by a full head, and she moved soundlessly.

They entered the hall. It was eerily silent here. The girl zigzagged from room to room, never stopping.

Elle wondered if this was some sort of a trap.

Was this girl a Klan member?

Then she put the thought out of her mind. She didn't have a choice.

"Stairs," the girl said, breathing hard. "Climb. Let's go."

The girl shoved an exit door open and they entered a cold stairwell. It was dark, and Elle had to feel her way up the stairs. She moved as quickly as she could, staying close to the girl, not wanting to get lost in the thick darkness.

They climbed until Elle's legs burned with the effort. The girl pushed through a door and sunlight seared Elle's vision. Her eyes filled with tears as she struggled to adjust to the light. The girl slammed the door shut.

They were on the roof.

And they weren't alone.

Elle took in her surroundings. The roof was big, overlooking the boulevard and the Santa Monica beach. They were at least twenty-five stories up. Three people were surrounding Elle. A tall, handsome young man with dark skin and glimmering brown eyes, and two Asian kids. A girl and a boy. They looked like twins.

"The Klan was going to kill her," the girl stated. She had a distinct southern accent. "I had to do something."

"She could be one of them," the young man said, glaring at Elle.

"She's not." The girl looked at Elle. "I'm right, aren't I?"

"I'm not an enemy," Elle said. "I'm a survivor."

"Great. So what do we do now?" The Asian girl spoke up. Her short, shiny black hair caught the sunlight. "Jay? What do we *do*?"

The young man peeked over the ledge of the building.

"I don't know," he said, never taking his gaze off Elle. "There's nowhere to go, unless you all want to jump."

"I don't think so," the frizzy blonde replied.

"They know we're up here," the Asian girl said.

"We can jump," Elle suggested.

The words felt heavy and clumsy on her lips. It had been a long time since she had spoken aloud.

"You're insane," the Asian girl said.

"No. I mean we could jump to the next building." Elle pointed. The roof couldn't be more than ten feet away from the next building. "They wouldn't expect that."

Hadn't she just done this stunt? This was only a few more feet.

"That's too dangerous," the young man - Jay - said.

Elle walked to the ledge. The Klan was gathering around the base of the building. In five or ten minutes, they would burst through the door on the roof, and they would all be dead. Elle had seen it happen to other survivors. The Klan showed no mercy.

"You can stay here," she shrugged. "I'm jumping."

She gauged the distance. She was small, light, and strong. She gave herself room to run and sprinted. The span between the two buildings was dizzying. The asphalt spun beneath her, twenty-five stories below. If she fell, she was dead. They would need an eraser to get her off the pavement.

She flew through the air.

And she came up an inch short. She hit the side of the ledge and slid, her fingers catching the edge of the building. She barely had a grip. Her fingers burned and her arms screamed with the effort. The kids on roof were yelling.

"Oh, my god! Pull up, kid!"

"She's freaking insane – I told you!"

Elle was terrified, hanging by her fingers twenty-five stories above the ground. She managed to pull herself up enough to get her forearm levered over the ledge. She hung for a moment, gathering her strength, then forced herself up, rolling over the ledge. She landed on the roof, smacking the side of her cheek as she hit.

She trembled as she sat up.

That was a close one. Too close.

Elle stood up. The kids on the other side of the building were staring at her. Awestruck? Probably not. They thought she was crazy.

"Okay," Jay said. "I guess I'm jumping, too."

He was tall, and his stride was impressive. Elle backed up and watched as he ran toward the ledge and launched himself over the gap, landing in a neat roll near her feet. He looked up at her, eyes sparking.

"You *are* insane," he said. "But good thinking, kid."

The frizzy blonde and the Asian twins followed suit. The Asian girl barely made it, but Jay caught her wrist before the girl could go tumbling to her death.

"You know a place where we could hide out, crazy girl?" the blonde asked Elle. "The Klan's on the hunt today. We need to lie low."

Elle thought about her question.

Should she help these kids? They could very well kill her the second she turned her back. Then again, they hadn't killed her *yet*, so that was a fairly positive sign.

"I know a place," she said.

Jay raised an eyebrow.

"Show us," he replied.

Elle nodded.

A rusty, decrepit fire escape stretched from the roof to the street. Elle swung her legs over the ledge and tested her weight on the metal platform. It shifted a little. She steadied herself and started climbing down. The other kids followed suit. Elle was faster than they were. She reached the bottom, tensely waiting for them to do the same.

"Now what?" the blonde whispered.

"Follow me," Elle replied.

She peeked her head around the corner of the building. There was no Klan in sight. They were probably making their way up the stairs of the other skyscraper, hoping to trap the kids on the roof.

"Run," Elle said.

She sprinted swiftly across the street, ducking into the next alley. She checked to make sure they had no pursuers. There was only the distant sound of the Klan's shouts as they barreled through the empty apartment building, searching for the children.

Chapter Four

Elle didn't take them home. Her apartment was her secret, and sharing it with total strangers would be stupid. Instead she took them to an old bakery. *La Fresh* was the name. It was a small shop hidden in an alleyway. At one point, Elle was sure that it had been trendy and hip. Now it was just impossible to find, camouflaged behind vines and creeping foliage.

Elle slipped through the front door. The brass bell on the door tinkled. Chairs and tables were mostly intact, but the glass case was empty. No more pastries. No more coffee.

"How did you know about this place?" Jay asked.

Elle didn't answer. She didn't trust them.

"We'll stay quiet until tomorrow morning," Elle said. "Then we can go our separate ways."

She backed into the corner of the kitchen. A broken coffeemaker lay on the floor.

"What's your name?" the blonde asked.

Elle cocked her head. Should she tell her? What harm could it do?

"Elle," she said.

"Like the letter?"

"Yeah." She held up her index finger and her thumb, making an L shape. "Elle for loser."

Jay smirked.

"I'm Georgia," the blonde said, thickening her southern accent for dramatic effect. "This is Flash." She gestured to the Asian boy, then to his sister. "This is his sister, Pix. And the tall loner in the corner is Jay."

"Somebody should keep a lookout," Elle said, "in case the Klan tracks us here."

"You know your way around the city," Jay stated, turning to Elle.

"We just got here," Georgia said, sitting on the counter. "I gotta say, this ain't the L.A. I was familiar with."

"Where did you all come from?" Elle asked.

"We were in a bunker. All of us." She gestured to the rest of the kids in the room. "There was a big group of us at the beginning. After the chemical weapons…well, some people went to the surface too soon. A lot of them…died." Georgia shrugged. "You can't fix stupid."

Elle blinked.

"You were in a bunker?" she asked. "For how long?"

"Until two months ago," Pix stated. She had a pretty, singsong accent. "We didn't know what we would find when we came up. The statistical probability of us finding an inhabitable urban environment-"

"-Don't get so technical, Pix," Jay interrupted. "The bunkers were underground. There were about twenty of us at the beginning – all young, like us. We had everything we needed. Food, water, radio contact, medicine. But it didn't last. Some went stir-crazy, and we ran out of supplies. The bunker was never meant to support twenty people. We lost almost everyone."

"Has the whole world gone crazy?" Georgia asked. "What's the rest of California like?"

Elle could see the fear in their eyes. The confusion. She couldn't imagine being locked away in the ground for a year, emerging into a world that was completely destroyed. It must have sucked.

"I don't know what the rest of the world is like," she said. "But I do know that most of California is dangerous like Los Angeles."

"What about the military?" Georgia asked. "I thought the United States was all-powerful or something."

"Apparently not," Elle shrugged. "What do you guys know about Omega?"

"Not much. Only that they're everywhere."

"Almost everywhere. They leave Hollywood and Santa Monica pretty much alone – they like to stay in Beverly Hills and downtown Los Angeles." Elle looked out the window. "I don't know who they are or where they came from, but they're bad. Really bad."

"We've only been in Hollywood for a week," Jay went on. "There's no food."

"There is if you know where to look," Elle replied, a sad smile spreading across her face. "Some food is safe to eat, as long as it's sealed. Don't eat anything that's been exposed to the air. The chemicals might have poisoned it. The same goes for water."

Georgia shared a sideways glance with Jay.

"You know a lot," Georgia said. "How do you stay alive all by yourself, shortstack?"

"I stay alive *because* I'm all by myself," Elle answered. "The Klan hunts in packs, and the only way to stay off their radar is if I'm smaller, quieter and faster than they are. Which I am. And that's why I'm still alive."

"I have a question for *you*," Elle said, turning the tables.

"Ask," Jay replied.

"What kind of a bunker were you guys hiding in? How many people were there? Were you there with your families or what?"

This time, it was Pix's twin brother, Flash, who answered:

"The bunker was built underneath a juvenile correctional facility. For emergencies. When Omega came, a lot of the kids in the facility died before we even made it into the bunker."

Elle released a frustrated sigh.

"So you were all in juvenile hall before Day Zero?" she asked.

"What's Day Zero?" Jay said.

"The day the power went out. When everything happened." Elle narrowed her gaze. "You didn't answer my question. Were you in jail?"

"Yeah, we were," Georgia said, tossing her hair back.

So. These children were orphaned juvenile delinquents. If Elle didn't trust them before, she sure as heck didn't trust them now.

"I hope none of you were wanted for murder," she grumbled as she retreated farther into the back of the building.

"Nah!" Georgia called. "I mean, *before* the Collapse? No. After?" A sly smile spread across her face. "Maybe."

Elle didn't believe her.

Like her mother always said, *Where there's smoke, there's firewater.*

"I don't want to go with him," Elle said. Tears were streaming down her face as she pleaded with her mother. She was standing in the kitchen. It was dark. The lights had been out for two days. Riots had begun in the city. Buildings were on fire. Women and children were begging for food in the gutters.

"You have to, Elle." Mother was a tall, willowy woman with black hair. "We don't have a choice. You don't, either. This is the only way to keep our family alive."

The kitchen was empty. The house was, too. It had been for a while.

When Dad and Johnny never came home...well, Elle's mother had gone off the deep end. Panic controlled her every move. And now she was sending Elle away, out of the city. To a place that was supposed to be safe.

Supposed to be.

"Why don't you come with me?" Elle begged.

"Because I have to wait for Daddy and Johnny."

"But they're not coming back, Mom. They're dead."

Mother slapped Elle across the face. Elle's cheek stung with pain, but she didn't cry out. She was too stubborn.

"Your uncle will take good care of you," Mother said, but her voice was venomous. She was angry. Mad that Elle had pointed out the obvious: Dad and Johnny were dead, and Mother was staying in the city because she wanted to die, too.

She was giving in.

"You're just going to give up," Elle whispered.

"I'm accepting the truth, Elle. Someday you'll understand."

"I'm going to come back for you," Elle promised.

*"Don't. Don't you **ever** come back to this city. This city is death."*

Elle shook her head.

"I will come back," she said. "I'll find you."

She meant every word.

Elle woke with a start. She was sitting upright in the corner of the bakery. Georgia and Jay were in the opposite corner, talking in low voices. Pix and Flash were asleep. She watched them. They were all thin, underfed. Elle wondered why they – out of all the kids at the juvenile correctional facility – had been the ones to survive.

They looked normal enough. They didn't appear to be hardened criminals. Pix and Flash couldn't be older than thirteen. Georgia looked to be around sixteen, and Jay was probably around seventeen or eighteen. They looked…tired. Like Elle.

She knew what it was like to be tired.

She toyed with the idea of bringing them home to her apartment, but decided against it. They could easily turn on her. So far, she had survived because she'd been smart. One stupid decision could end her life.

She wasn't about to start a bad habit now.

She got to her feet and walked toward Georgia and Jay. They immediately stopped talking, piquing Elle's curiosity.

"What's up?" she asked.

Georgia hesitated.

"Well. We were thinking," she whispered. "Maybe since you know so much about the city, you could give us some tips. Like where to find food. We're starving, Elle. We need help."

Elle looked at Jay. He seemed frustrated to be asking for help. "We just want to know what you know," he said, tense. "Where to look for food. What areas to avoid. That kind of thing. It might keep us alive longer."

Elle raised an eyebrow.

"You want a tip?" she remarked. "Here's one: get out of the city. There's nothing here for you. If starvation or sickness doesn't get you, the Klan will. And if for some reason you avoid all three of those things, you've got to deal with Omega. You're already dead, you just don't know it yet."

"But *you* survived here, shortstack," Georgia countered. "So can we."

"I'm lucky."

"You know what you're doing."

"And my life could end in a second! All I have to do is make one mistake and I'm dead." Elle felt the color rush to her cheeks. "You need to understand that everything in this city is death. Almost every building is full of rotting bodies and most of the food was poisoned when the chemical weapon hit the city. The Klan executes foragers like me on the streets and hangs their dead bodies from lampposts to mark their territory. This isn't a city anymore, this is a battlefield. And sooner or later, all the good guys are going to be dead."

Jay and Georgia stared at her, their jaws slack.

Elle swallowed, uncomfortable. She hadn't meant to go on a rant, but they needed to grasp the danger that the city held.

"If it's so dangerous, why haven't you left?" Jay asked, his dark gaze searing into hers.

Elle didn't know what to say. She didn't have an answer.

"It's morning," she said instead. "I need to go."

"Elle, please help us," Georgia pleaded, standing from the table.

"You don't need my help. You need to get out."

"But we have nowhere to go!"

Elle lifted her shoulder in a halfhearted shrug, throwing her hood over her head. "Join the club," she commented.

"Please, Elle. Jay won't say it, but I will: we need your help, and we're begging you." Georgia touched Elle's arm. Elle flinched. "We haven't eaten in three days."

Elle closed her eyes.

She knew what it was like to be hungry. To be starving.

"If I help you," she said, "then you have to promise to let me leave when I'm done. You can't follow me."

Georgia nodded.

"We can do that." She looked at Jay. "Right?"

Jay stood up and offered his hand. Elle just stared at it.

"You can trust us, Elle," he said. "We're not bad people. We're not here to hurt you."

Elle dropped her gaze to the floor.

She'd heard people say that before…

She said, "I can show you where to find a little food and water."

"That's all we need," Georgia answered.

Elle wanted to shake her, to tell her NO. They needed to leave the city. That's what they *really* needed.

But she didn't.

Jay stood in the shadows, a muscle ticking in his strong jaw. He looked like he could be twenty years old, but if he had been in a juvenile correctional facility only last year, he couldn't be older than eighteen.

Flash and Pix groggily awoke.

They'll have to wake up faster than that if they want to stay alive here, Elle thought. *The Klan doesn't give you time to be lazy.*

"First lesson," Elle said, tightening the straps on her backpack. "Sleep wide awake. The Klan is everywhere, and there's more of them than us. So. Don't be lazy."

"Sleep awake?" Pix echoed. "That makes no sense."

Elle shook her head.

This was going to be more effort than it was worth.

Nadia's Market was an organic grocery store before Day Zero. Movie stars and wealthy socialites would shop there, buying bags of lentils and quinoa, and other staples of an elite's diet. Unfortunately, the organic food didn't last as long as the processed foods, and that was Elle's first lesson to the kids.

"The only thing you'll find in there are jars of almond butter," she said. "And that's not a bad thing; I mean, food is food. But you're better off spending your time searching somewhere else."

They were standing catty corner to the market. The parking lot was full of rusty, broken shopping carts. A colony of once-elegant penthouse apartments comprised the neighborhood around them.

"Where are the birds?" Georgia asked. Her tall frame was sitting on the curb. She stared at the sky. "There are no seagulls, no bugs. Where is everything?"

"Seagulls are starting to come back to the beach," Elle stated. "Everything else is dead."

"Are we breathing poison right now?" Jay asked.

"The probability of that scenario is slim," Pix piped up, pulling her red beanie around her forehead. "More likely than not, Omega launched chemical rockets at the city that killed the population with Sarin gas. It kills on contact with the skin, but it doesn't linger in the air."

"One and done," Georgia deadpanned, pulling a cigarette out of her jacket pocket. She lit it with a match, took a drag, and puffed the smoke into the air. "Omega knows what they're doing, you can't argue with that."

Elle nodded.

"Yeah," she said. "Besides, Omega wouldn't have come back to the city if they were going to be poisoned by their own weapons."

"You sure about that?" Jay asked.

"Pretty sure."

"Maybe we just haven't been affected yet."

Elle rolled her eyes. "I would be dead by now if that was the case," she said. "Come on. Follow me."

"Three cheers for Follow the Leader," Georgia drawled.

Elle led them away from *Nadia's Market,* two blocks backward. The sky was cloudy today. It looked like it might rain again.

"Where do you live?" Jay asked.

Elle gave him a look.

"Okay, okay." Jay threw his hands up. "I was just asking a question, kid."

Elle didn't like being called kid. In fact, she didn't like talking to Jay at all. He didn't seem to relish being given tips by a girl that was about half his size. But he needed her to survive, and that gave Elle a little bit of satisfaction.

"There," Elle said, stopping. "We're here."

They followed Elle into an alleyway. She paused at a garbage can halfway down the street. She pushed it aside, revealing a small door. It was rusty and looked abandoned.

The kids looked confused.

Elle opened the door. It creaked. She stepped down. It was cold and damp. She descended down a flight of steps, stopping in complete darkness. She grabbed a flashlight from her backpack and flicked it on.

"That looks dangerous," Flash whispered.

He wore wiry round glasses that balanced on the tip of his nose. He pushed them up and looked at Elle. "Is this secure?" he stated from the opening.

"It was the last time I was here," Elle said. "Come on."

"What is this place?" Jay asked. None of the kids were moving.

"It's a *cache*." Elle shined the flashlight in Jay's face. "Are you going to make me do this alone, or do I have to drag you guys down here?"

Jay grimaced. He hesitantly climbed down the steps. Georgia, Flash and Pix followed suit. Elle handed Jay her spare flashlight.

"Stay quiet," Elle whispered.

The room was wide, packed with stacks of pallets on which were canned goods and packaged containers of food, like ramen noodles and fruit cocktail.

"Oh, my god," Georgia muttered. "How did you find this place, shortstack?"

"A few weeks ago," Elle explained. "It was somebody's hidden cache, and I'm guessing they're dead, because they haven't been back." Elle paused. "I've been adding to the supplies myself. I won't eat anything unless I can replace it."

"Is it safe?" Pix asked.

Elle gave her a look.

"Of course not," Elle replied.

Elle slid between two rows of pallets, next to Flash. The boy was staring at a pile of canned vegetables.

"Why do they call you Flash?" Elle whispered. "Are you a fast runner or something?"

The boy touched one of the cans, a glazed expression on his face.

He was starving. Elle could see it.

"No," he replied. "Flash. Like the flash drive for a computer."

"You're good with computers?"

Flash grinned slightly.

"Yeah. A little."

The silence was cut by the sound of Georgia's piercing scream.

Chapter Five

Elle's head echoed with Georgia's shriek. She sprinted to the other side of the basement storeroom. The girl was pressed against the wall, grabbing Jay's arm. They were staring at something on the ground.

It was a dead body. A woman. A puddle of dried, pungent blood had pooled beneath the base of her skull. She'd been shot in the head. Her body was just beginning to smell.

"What the hell kind of a place is *this*?" Georgia breathed.

Elle spun around and held a finger to her lips. Hadn't she told these idiots to be quiet? But did they listen? No.

Elle took a cautious step forward and peered at the woman's head. She was middle age, salt-and-pepper hair cut to the chin. There was a small red dot in the center of her forehead. A perfect kill shot.

"Somebody's been trying to steal my stuff," Elle whispered.

"I say we get out of here," Georgia replied.

"And do what? Let whoever shot this lady take all of this food?" Elle shook her head. "No way. I need this food to stay alive – and so do you, now that you're here."

Something rustled at the far end of the basement. Elle dropped to the ground, behind a pallet stacked with food. Flash and Pix huddled close to her, with Georgia and Jay right behind them.

"What is it?" Jay hissed. "Elle?"

Fear coiled in the pit of her stomach.

"Someone's inside," she whispered.

She nodded toward the other side of the basement, where she'd heard the noise.

"Let's go," Pix said. Her tiny voice was trembling. "Please."

"And leave the *food* to someone else?" Elle demanded.

"Is it worth dying over?" Jay pointed out. "We should go."

But Elle was already moving. She crawled on the floor, hiding behind pallets. She drew her bowie knife from her hip sheath, keeping a firm grip on the handle. She flicked her flashlight off, listening, controlling her breathing. The kids still had their flashlight on, illuminating a shred of the basement. She saw a flicker of a shadow on the far back wall.

Ah, there you are.

Whoever was inside was trying to stay hidden, too. At some point Jay recovered from his shock and realized that his flashlight was like a beacon, leading the invaders in the basement straight to their position. He flicked the light off, and all was dark, silent.

Elle didn't move. She strained her ears for a noise, a tiny indication of human presence. She sat there for several tense minutes, sweat running down her forehead. She heard a shuffling noise, like someone was slowly moving around the far side of the pallet a few feet in front of her. She gripped her knife.

Bam!

The stack of canned vegetables collapsed next to Elle's shoulder, toppling over her head. She covered her neck with her hands as the tower rained down, leaving bruises. The metal cans hit the cement. It sounded like something had exploded inside the basement. Elle felt her body being shoved aside. It took her just a split second to realize that some*one* was touching her.

She instinctively grabbed at the figure. She couldn't see anything, but she felt a leg. She tightened her fingers around the material of a pant-leg and slashed up with her knife. There was a yelp of pain, and the figure collapsed on the pile of scattered cans. Elle slashed again. Whoever it was – a man, Elle guessed – kicked back, slamming Elle's small body against another pallet. More cans fell down.

From inside the basement, someone screamed.

It sounded like Pix.

Elle rolled to her side, her ribcage throbbing from the impact of the kick. The silent fight continued as the man grabbed her by the hair and yanked her forward. Pieces of hair tore out of Elle's scalp. She lifted her knife and shoved it forward, sinking into flesh. There was a strangled scream as the hands released her hair. She fell, pulling the knife toward her, feeling it glide through bone and cartilage.

Elle backed away, feeling her way toward the struggle in the back of the basement. The flashlight had been flicked on again, and it was lying sideways on the floor. Elle glimpsed a shadow of Jay struggling against a bigger man. It was impossible to make out faces, but she guessed the man was middle age. Georgia ran forward and pushed off the wall, snapping her boot into the man's shoulder. He bent over with the hit and Jay shoved his fist into his face.

There were three more people in the back of the storeroom, and the basement door had been opened. More were coming inside.

The cache had been completely infiltrated.

Elle was furious.

"We have to go!" she told Jay. "Now!"

They were sorely outnumbered.

"Alright, kiddies!" someone yelled. It was a male voice, deep and raspy. "Time to stop with the playground antics. One of my men is dead, and that's not something I'm willing to overlook." A pause. "Why don't you just walk to the front of the room and surrender? We won't hurt you, I promise."

Sure, they won't hurt us, Elle thought. *They'll only kill us.*

She knelt and grabbed the flashlight, flicking the switch off again. The only light in the basement was the stream of sunlight coming in through the entrance. Three people were standing on the steps.

"Come out, come out wherever you are," the man drawled.

Elle felt Georgia's hand in the darkness. She leaned close to her head and whispered, "We have to draw them into the basement, then we'll dash for the door."

Georgia relayed the message to the others.

"I know you're in here," the man said. "Let's not make this harder than it has to be. We won't hurt you. We'll give you a home. A place with food and water. How does that sound?"

Elle wanted to *show* him how that sounded, but she knew better.

She rounded the back end of the basement, tiptoeing around pallets. The kids followed suit. Elle silently instructed them to separate across the storeroom. She stayed where she was, almost directly in front of the basement steps.

The man kept talking, trying to draw the kids out of the basement, to the front of the room. Elle knew what he was doing; he was lulling them into a sense of false security, weakening their defenses. She slowly unzipped her backpack and reached inside, feeling for the right object…yes, there it was.

"If you come out now, we'll give you a nice home at the Pits," the man said.

At this, Elle froze. A chill ran up her spine.

"You'll be taken care of."

You lying dog, Elle thought. *The Klan will never take me again.*

Elle dug for the lighter in the bottom of her pack. She found it. Her hands were shaky; she willed them to cooperate. She flicked her thumb along the roller and the flame ignited. She was holding a box in the other hand – a box with a fuse.

Elle threw the package toward the steps, dropped the lighter back into her pack, and covered her head. The box exploded, sending sprays of fiery color into the basement. The men on the steps dove for cover, and one of them was knocked off his feet. The colored balls of fire kept popping, rattling the basement, creating chaos.

Firecrackers. One of Elle's favorite post-apocalyptic weapons.

Elle sprinted toward the exit, climbing the stairs with lightning speed. She charged into the alley, the daylight burning her eyes. She glanced behind her. Jay was next, and then Georgia. Elle fixed her gaze straight ahead and kept running. They needed to hide.

The screams of the men in the basement didn't fade until they were two blocks away. Elle slowed her pace a bit, but she didn't stop until they were safely on the other side of the city, near Santa Monica Boulevard again.

She placed her hands on her knees, breathing hard. She was hidden behind an overflowing garbage can in the alley near an abandoned Mexican restaurant. Jay and Georgia came to a halt beside her. Elle reached up and touched her shirt. She was dripping in blood – not hers, but the man who she had stabbed inside the basement.

"Flash, where's Pix?" Georgia gasped.

Georgia's hair was mussed and her shirt was torn. Jay's knuckles were bloody; Elle could see a piece of white bone protruding through the skin.

Flash leaned against the alley wall, struggling for breath. His glasses were sideways. "She was…right behind…me," he panted.

Elle stood up. Pix was nowhere in sight.

"Did she make it out of the basement?" Elle asked.

"Yeah, I saw her come out," Jay replied. "I didn't check afterward, though. I was…running…" He seemed embarrassed. "I thought she was with Flash."

As Flash regained his breath, it seemed to dawn on him that his sister was missing. "Pix?" he called.

"Shhhh," Georgia hissed. "Dummy! Do you want the whole posse to come down on us again?"

Elle frowned.

They had no idea what had just happened.

Elle waited. Her heart rate slowed. Her fight or flight instinct vanished, and she crouched low, watching the street. They all watched, hoping Pix had just fallen behind and that she would catch up.

Elle counted the minutes. One, two, three….five…seven.

Too long.

"She's not coming," Elle stated. "They got her."

"*Who* got her?" Jay demanded. "What *was* that, anyway? A basement full of food *and* thugs? We almost *died* down there, Elle!"

"Welcome to the city," Elle replied.

"We can't just leave her behind!" Flash said, eyes wide. "She's my sister!"

"We can and we will," Elle replied. "Do you know who that *was* in the storeroom? The Klan. We can't *mess* with the Klan."

"But they've got Pix!"

And she was as good as dead, if Elle was right.

Chapter Six

They were hiding out in a tiny, single-level apartment living room. The curtains were drawn and they spoke in whispers. They had backtracked as far as they dared, searching for Pix. There was no sign.

"Is she…dead?" Flash breathed.

They were sitting on the cold, damp floor.

"I heard that big guy in the basement say something about 'The Pits,'" Georgia said. "He said he wanted to take us there. What is that?"

"Is that where they took Pix?" Flash asked, a spark of hope on his face.

"If it is," Elle replied, "she's dead."

Jay demanded, " Why? Have you heard of the Pits?"

"Yeah, I've heard of them."

"What are they?"

Elle grimaced. "It's a Klan game," she said. "They throw prisoners into big pits in the ground and make them fight. To the death. Klan members bet against each other – not with money, but with gold, guns or supplies. It's bad. *Very* bad."

"They're taking my sister there?" Flash whispered. He was trembling. Jay and Georgia looked equally distressed. Elle just stared at them, thinking.

"They round up anyone they can find," Elle answered. "Men, women and children. If you get taken to the pits, you've been given a death sentence. Nobody survives for very long."

"What's the *point* of that?" Flash sniffled. "Why do they do it?"

"Because they can," Elle replied. "This is the world we live in, now."

"You don't seem too concerned about this," Georgia snapped.

Elle shrugged.

"Sorry, but Pix is gone."

"No. We have to rescue her," Jay cut in. "We can't let her die."

"You have to," Elle told him. "The Klan has her. There's nothing you can do now."

"Where are the Pits?" Flash asked quietly. His eyes were red, but he hadn't shed a tear. Not yet. "Do you know where we can find them?"

"You don't want to go to the Pits," Elle stated, "unless you have a death wish."

"We're not leaving Pix to the Klan," Jay answered.

Elle was dumbfounded. These kids would really go on a suicidal rescue mission to save one person from their group? Didn't they know any better?

She was annoyed, but deep down, she was impressed. Something deeper than mere survival instinct held this group together. Something stronger.

"The Klan outnumbers you a hundred to one," Elle pointed out.

"We have to try," Jay replied.

"You really *are* clueless," Elle answered.

"Please, Elle," Georgia interjected. "You don't have to come with us. We're just asking you to tell us where it is…if you know."

Elle met Georgia's piercing blue eyes. She weighed her options. She could take off right now and leave these kids behind her, never thinking about them again. She had already wasted enough time trying to teach them how to find food – and look what had happened. They'd almost gotten killed.

Or she could tell them where the Pits were, and they would leave. Of course, they would die, because the Pits were in Klan territory and a group of naïve bunker survivors didn't stand a chance of pulling off a successful rescue. Either way, Elle didn't have to worry about them anymore. They'd be out of sight, and out of mind.

But as Flash stood there on shaky feet, Jay's strong arm around his tiny shoulders, something grabbed her heart. For the first time since she'd come to the city, she felt *sympathy*. It had been a long time since she'd felt anything for anyone…even herself. Her world was cold and dark. Unfeeling.

"I can show you where it is," Elle said at last. "But don't expect to come out of this alive."

She wasn't being cruel. She was just being honest.

"Thank you," Georgia breathed. "This means a lot."

Elle shook her head.

Georgia had no idea.

The Klan's territory spread through Hollywood, Culver City, Santa Monica and Malibu. Elle had spent months exploring the abandoned segments of the city, the parts that weren't under Omega's strict control. She knew every street, every building. She knew where the

Klan spent most of their time, and she knew how they thought. How they operated.

"How far?" Georgia asked.

They had been walking for a long time. Elle shook her head.

"A while," she answered.

Georgia sighed.

Flash hadn't said a word since they'd left, and it was late afternoon.

Elle tried to talk to him.

"So, you're nicknamed after a flash drive," she said. "Why?"

Flash shrugged.

"My sister and I...we spent a lot of time on computers."

"Doing what?"

He didn't answer right away. Then, "Learning."

From the tone of his voice, Elle had a feeling there was a lot more to the story than he was willing to talk about.

"You were in juvenile hall," Elle said. "Were you a hacker?"

Flash looked up sharply, a mysterious light coming to his eyes.

"Maybe," he replied. "Maybe we were."

He refused to pursue the conversation, plunged deep into his own fear of losing his sister to the Klan. Elle lapsed into silence again. She didn't feel like talking anymore.

As they moved through the city, Elle became more uptight. Every creak, every echo was suspicious. They were deep into Klan territory.

"Where are we going?" Georgia whispered, falling into step with Elle. "Elle? Please talk to us."

Elle felt a twinge of guilt, keeping them in the dark like this. She wasn't used to negotiating social situations, and her conversational skills were...lacking. She turned to Georgia and said, "The Pits are right in the heart of Klan territory. Like, the dead center. We just follow this road-" she pointed to a street sign that said *Sunset Boulevard,* "-and take it to North Highland Avenue."

"Street names don't mean anything to me," Jay muttered.

"Well, they better," Elle replied. "Pay attention to your surroundings. You never know when you might get lost." She turned to Georgia. "So to answer your question, we're about a mile and a half away."

Elle was hoping that once they actually saw the Pits, they would abandon their plan to rescue Pix. Because the Pits, to Elle at least, represented hell itself.

The time dragged by. Moving quietly and slowly, it seemed to take an eternity to reach their destination. As they drew closer to the Pits, signs of Klan inhabitation became obvious. Buildings had been painted with the Klan symbol; a blood red X. Each point of the X looked like an arrow. It symbolized death and destruction.

It symbolized a new era of neo-civilization. A barbaric society.

Windows were painted with the X. Old billboards were covered with giant red X symbols. The boulevard widened and the street had been painted with big, red letters:

INTRUDERS BEWARE

TRESPASSING = DEATH

Below the words, blood stained the road. Elle turned to the others. Jay and Georgia looked terrified.

"You still want to go through with this?" Elle asked.

They didn't answer. She took that as a yes.

They continued. They traveled under a freeway overpass. The bottom of the road and the support beams for the highway were covered in graffiti. Bright, vulgar phrases and warnings were painted along the walls and ceiling. Grotesque artwork snarled at them.

"Don't look," Elle warned. "It's bad."

But it was too late. Jay, Georgia and Flash were staring at the graffiti, mesmerized. Elle hurried on, reaching the end of the tunnel. An off ramp from the freeway slid onto a large boulevard. There was a park here. It was pretty – maybe the only pretty thing left in the entire city.

Elle dropped to a crouch behind a wall of foliage. There was a huge park up ahead. Barbed wire wound haphazardly around the outside of the park, dotted with sharp, pointed stakes. It was archaic. A sign sat on a protruding piece of concrete, once prominent in the never-ceasing flow of Los Angeles traffic. The words were difficult to make out.

"You've *got* to be kidding me," Georgia hissed.

"Welcome to the Pits," Elle whispered.

They had reached the Pits:

The Hollywood Bowl.

Chapter Seven

The Hollywood Bowl belonged to the Klan. From their vantage point near the off ramp, Elle and the kids could see the tip of the half dome that enclosed the world-famous stage. The seats around the stage were filled with hundreds of Klan members. They were screaming and yelling, throwing trash and bottles and crude comments. A huge bonfire lit the scene, tossing distorted, leaping shadows across the stage.

"The big stage is where they pit the toughest fighters against each other," Elle explained.

"What about the Pits?" Georgia whispered, horrified. "Where are those?"

"Behind the Bowl," Elle replied. "Come on. Follow me, and this time, do *exactly* what I tell you. The Klan has a lot more security than you'd think."

Gang members roved the border of the park, patrolling, looking for people that dared trespass on their territory.

Elle stopped dead in her tracks. Georgia bumped into her back, pushing her forward. Elle barely regained her balance. She shot

Georgia a harsh glare, gesturing ahead. Two Klan members were coming their way. They were loud, stomping along, talking in slurred voices. Clearly drunk.

Elle slid into a bush and the kids followed.

"...Come on, Elena," the first of the two Klan members said. A male. "We're missing it."

"I'm coming, I'm *coming*."

"I've got a lot riding on this fight. Hurry up."

"I'm hurrying..."

They passed slowly, but as soon as they were out of sight, Elle crawled out of the cover of the bush and looked around. Evening was setting in, masking the park in shadows. Torches were being lit, giving the area a tribal appearance.

"This place gives me the creeps," Georgia muttered.

It should, Elle thought.

Jay and Flash said nothing, but Elle noticed Jay's hand on the thirteen-year old boy's forearm. Jay sensed her stare and Elle looked away, embarrassed.

I'm just not used to people, she thought. *There's nothing to feel weird about.*

They came around the back of the park. It was quieter here, and the reason was obvious. Huge, animalistic kennels had been set up between the trees. People were crammed between trees, enclosed on all sides with sheets of cyclone fencing. Some of them held a single person – prize fighters – and others were filled with groups of prisoners.

Just beyond the cages, huge, muddy pits had been dug into the ground.

They were the small fighting arenas – *the* Pits.

"Who are these prisoners?" Georgia commented, frowning. "Gladiators?"

"Basically," Elle replied.

"Bunch of maniacs, if you ask me." Georgia took a deep breath – apparently she was more rattled by the sight than she wanted to admit. "Remind me *never* to visit Hollywood again."

Elle fought the urge to turn back, to run away. This place brought back memories. Very bad memories.

Why am I here? Why am I doing this?

Again, she had no answer. It just felt like the right thing to do, she guessed.

"The Pits are just beyond where they keep the prisoners," Elle whispered.

"Where will Pix be?" Flash asked.

"I don't know. She could be in any of the cages."

"How are we going to find her without being seen?"

"I'm working on it."

Elle studied the area. The cages were lined up in two rows parallel to each other. Klan guards roamed between the cages, keeping watch. They carried long, pointed stakes. Occasionally one of them would shove the stake through the cyclone fencing and harass the prisoners, keeping them subdued.

"This is going to have to be insanely fast," Elle said. "You're going to have to trust me."

"I'm not sure we can pull this off," Jay replied, hesitant.

"Hey, you're the ones who wanted to come here," Elle pointed out.

"I know. But this…we don't stand a chance."

Elle sighed. Hadn't she tried to tell him this before they came?

"Well, I'm here now, and I'm not leaving until I do some damage," Elle snorted. "You can leave if you want to."

Weird how the tables had turned. Seeing this place had reminded Elle how much she hated the Klan – how much she wished somebody would take them down.

"I have to help Pix," Flash said, his voice soft.

"Well, I didn't walk a mile down Sunset Boulevard and a thousand empty pawn shops to sit on my butt and do nothing," Georgia replied. "I'm still in."

Jay didn't say a word.

"We need a diversion," Elle said, narrowing her eyes at Jay. "Pix could be in any of the cages, and the only way we'll have enough time to find her is if we open *all* of them."

"You're *insane*," Jay stated.

"You've told me that before," Elle replied. "Trust me, I know what I'm talking about. Jay and Flash, you create a diversion. A big one. Blow up something. See that bonfire on this side of the Pits? There are diesel tanks that they use to keep the torches burning." She pointed. "See? Make a huge fire or explosion. Make it loud."

"How do you know where to find all of this stuff?" Georgia asked.

"Georgia, you come with me," she said, ignoring the question. "As soon as Jay and Flash blow up the tanks, these Klan members standing guard are going rush over there. We'll have a chance to open the cages, if we're lucky."

"And then what? There are hundreds of Klan members in the arena around the corner," Jay said. "We're toast."

"We're going to run, and then we're going to hide," Elle answered. "And we're going to stay hidden until the Klan calms down. Then we move on."

"What if they capture us?" Georgia asked after a long silence.

"Then we're dead."

"If we separate from Jay and Flash, how are we going to meet up with them again?"

"We'll have a meeting place," Elle said. "Do you remember the bakery where we stayed last night? We'll meet there. It's far away from here and it's hidden." She turned to Jay. "Can you find the bakery on your own?"

Jay shrugged. Elle didn't find that very reassuring.

"Any questions?" Elle offered.

Georgia raised her hand like a kid in a classroom. The gesture almost made Elle laugh.

Almost.

"How do we get the cages open?" Georgia asked.

"We cut the wire," Elle said, pointing to the coil of wire twisted around the cyclone fencing. Elle drew a pair of wire cutters from her backpack. "I'm always prepared," she grinned.

Then Elle pointed to a thickset, tall man with a shaved head. His forehead and cheeks were swirling with tattoos. He wore no shirt, just combat fatigues and a leather strap across his chest. The strap sheathed a sword on his back.

"He's our biggest problem," Elle whispered. "He's the chief guard. He gives the orders. You can tell by his tattoo, see?" The man had the Klan symbol tattooed on his left bicep. "We take him out, and some of our worst problems are eliminated."

"Please tell me you're joking," Georgia sighed.

"I could," Elle said, "but it would be a lie."

"He's huge. He's like an anvil with legs."

"I'll take care of him. You focus on cutting the wire." Elle handed Georgia the wire cutters. "You've got be quick."

Jay interjected, "We're probably going to die, aren't we?"

Elle wanted to slap him. Yes, she'd known that this was probably a suicide mission, but that was before she had decided to help them. She had planned to lead them here and let them pull off the rescue attempt on their own.

But something inside her wouldn't let her do that.

She wanted to do something about the cages sitting in front of her. She wanted to help. The world might be destroyed and society might have collapsed – but she could do a little good. She could help someone.

"You ready?" Elle said.

No one answered.

Elle took that as a yes.

"They're all dead, Elle."

Uncle stood in the doorway of the ranch house, tall and imposing. His scraggly gray hair hung limply to his shoulders. Rain drops slid down his wrinkled face. Elle sat on the floor, a book in her hands.

"Mom can't be dead," Elle stated. "She was supposed to wait for us."

"I know. But she wasn't there."

"So she could still be alive, then."

"My girl, your mother is gone, and so is your father and your brother." Uncle took a step closer, and Elle was suddenly on her feet, drawing back. "Please, Elle. Listen to what I'm saying: they're gone. You need to accept this. Life won't get any easier until you do."

"Life sucks," Elle said, blinking back tears. "We're living in hiding – people are dying all around us. There's nothing left! It's not going to get easier. **Ever**."

Uncle's eyes were red, as if he had been crying.

Elle remembered when the power had gone out, when everything had gone dark forever. She remembered the panic, the riots. The massacres and the whispers of a shadow army on the coastline. Her father and her brother, slipping out one night to find food. Her mother waiting at the window of their apartment in Beverly Hills, sitting there for three days. Sending Elle away with Uncle, into the hills, away from the city.

"She has to be there, somewhere," Elle said.

"Hope is a good thing," Uncle replied, "but in this case, accept the truth. Your family is dead, but you have us. You have your Aunt and I. You're not alone."

Elle threw her book into the fireplace. The flames consumed the pages, slowly eating away the words. She stared at it until it was a pile of charred, black debris. Uncle placed a hand on Elle's shoulder. She shook it off.

Uncle was wrong. Mom had to be alive.

Johnny and Daddy were dead, but Mom...

She had to go back. She had to find her.

And Uncle couldn't stop her.

Elle's palms were sweaty. She waited with Georgia on the far side of the park, staring at the long rows of cages. The prisoners were filthy, caked in mud and dried blood. They sat and stared into space with vacant expressions.

"What the hell is wrong with people?" Georgia whispered. "This is barbaric."

This is life, Elle thought bitterly.

"Remember, leave the big guy to me," Elle replied. "You get those cages open and look for Pix. Then we're out of here."

"Okay, okay," Georgia replied. Then, "Why are you helping us, Elle? You've really got no reason to."

Elle frowned.

"I don't know," she said.

"Liar," Georgia observed, lifting an eyebrow. "There's something here that you want."

Elle blinked, startled at Georgia's perceptiveness.

But she didn't answer. She didn't like to talk about the past with people that she didn't trust completely. Not that she thought Georgia was out to kill her, but still…information was valuable. She didn't want to give it away so easily.

"Okay, they've *got* to be ready by now," Elle muttered.

Jay and Flash needed to hurry up. The chief guard was walking closer, pacing up and down between the cages. This was their opportunity.

Come on, hurry up!

The explosion caught Elle off guard. It was huge. The diesel tanks roared into towering flames and detonated like bombs, flattening the foliage around them instantly. Heat burned Elle's face and singed the hair on her arms. She shielded her eyes. The roar from the inferno was constant, like a waterfall. A wave of sound. Flames licked around the tops of the trees and seared the grass. Klan members lay twisted at unnatural angles on the ground, their skin charred and black.

Several guards were caught in the explosion. They struggled to regain their balance. Elle heard screaming and cursing. The chief guard slowly got to his feet, bewildered by shock and the blistering flames.

Even Elle's ears were ringing.

"Here we go," she told Georgia.

And then she was gone. She sprinted out of the cover of the foliage and ran between the cages, making a beeline for the head guard. The prisoners in the cages were watching the explosion, eyes wide.

One of the guards had dropped a stake after the explosion. It lay on the ground, untouched. Elle grabbed it as she flashed past. She came up behind the chief guard and slammed the blunt tip into the soft spot in the back of his skull with the full force of her running momentum. His huge, brawny body dropped like a sack of rocks.

She reached down and grabbed the sword on his back, drawing the gleaming blade in an arc around her head. Elle fastened the leather strap around her chest, sheathed the word and looked up, searching for Georgia. The tall girl was feverishly cutting through the wires on the second cage. The prisoners were pushing against the cyclone fencing, frenzied. Escape!

"RUN!" Elle shouted. "You're free – get out and don't come back!"

The prisoners pushed out of the first two cages, almost knocking Georgia and Elle underfoot in the process.

"Okay, I'll cut," Elle said, grabbing the wire cutters. "You look for Pix!"

"PIX?" Georgia yelled. "Pix? Where are you?!?"

There were just under a dozen cages here. Elle worked fast to cut the wires before the full force of Klan guards returned. If they were caught – especially Elle – there would be hell to pay.

"Elle!"

Pix's small, pale face peeked through the bars of the last cage in the row. It was stuffed with younger children. Elle unlocked the door and the children flooded outside. Screams of joy and gratitude filled the air.

"Run!" Elle kept yelling. "You have to GET OUT!"

Stupid people! Didn't they realize the clock was ticking?

Bam!

Something slammed into Elle's shoulder. She saw stars. The world exploded in a burst of color as she tumbled to the ground, her shoulder throbbing with pain. She rolled to her feet, lost her balance, and grabbed the side of a cage to stand. The man who she had taken the sword from was standing there, and he was enraged.

"Elle," the man snarled. "Well, well. What have we here? You've come back."

A stone dropped to the pit of Elle's stomach. Out of the corner of her eye, she saw Georgia grab Pix's arm and take off into the night.

"I'm leaving, Tomas," Elle spat. "Get out of my way."

"You're not going anywhere." Tomas's expression became feral. "You'll pay for this."

"Don't think so," Elle heaved, still wracked with pain.

She pulled her handgun out of her belt and pointed it at his face. She took a step backward.

"You won't shoot me," Tomas laughed, taking a step forward. "You never had it in you to kill. That's why you failed in the Pits, girl. It takes a killer to be a prize fighter."

"I've killed Klan members before," Elle replied, standing her ground. "And I'll kill you, too."

Her hands shook as she held the gun. She willed herself to remain steady, to make sure the safety was off. She had to do this; she had to kill Tomas. He deserved nothing less than death for everything that he had done.

Crack!

Tomas's head jerked violently forward. Blood sprayed across Elle's face. She stood there, shocked, her finger still on the trigger. She hadn't fired a shot. What had happened?

"Elle!" Jay bounded out of the shadows, Flash in tow. He ran to her, shook her shoulders. He shoved a handgun into his belt. "Are you okay?"

"You shot him," she said, numb.

"Yes. Come on, we've to go. Now!"

He took Elle's arm and dragged her away from Tomas's lifeless body. After a few seconds, Elle regained control of her emotions and yanked her arm out of Jay's grip.

"Where did you get a *gun*?" she snapped.

"I've had one the whole time," Jay grinned.

"You're an idiot." She shot him a sideways glance. "Thanks."

Jay laughed. Elle didn't know how to respond.

It had been *ages* since she'd heard laughter.

So she tucked her head, holstered her gun, and the three of them followed the flood of escapees into the night, disappearing into the darkness of Klan territory.

Chapter Eight

Elle wasn't born into killing, she was thrown into it. She had been the daughter of an actress and a man who owned an organic health store. Her fifteen year-old brother had been a violinist. And Elle? She was a gymnastics competitor and a martial arts enthusiast. She didn't start off as a survivor...but maybe, in some strange way, she had been preparing for life after Day Zero since she was born.

Martial arts, gymnastics, survival skills. These are things that had saved her life in the city. Things that a lot of people didn't know or couldn't pull off.

She was lucky, and she knew it.

Elle, Jay and Flash ran through the night. They had become separated from Georgia and Pix when the Pits had erupted into total chaos. The flames from the explosive diesel tanks had spread to the trees and the grass. It was eating away at the park, and the Klan was scrambling to contain the blaze.

Elle felt a rush of satisfaction.

Good, she thought. *I hope the Pits are completely destroyed.*

The prisoners that escaped from the cages were dispersing throughout the city. Some of them were recaptured by the Klan – but most of them got away. As they got farther away from the Pits, they slowed their pace. Elle's muscles were burning, her throat was dry, and she was still shaken from facing down Tomas.

"That man," Jay panted. "You knew him. You were a prisoner in the Pits."

Elle said nothing. She didn't need to.

"Why didn't you just kill him?" he asked.

Elle grabbed Flash's shoulder and pulled the younger child away from the corner of a building. She made sure it was clear, and they continued.

"I don't know," Elle replied.

"But you told Tomas that you had killed Klan members."

Elle picked up the pace again. "Klan members don't count as humans. They're just shadows of who they used to be. So it can't be murder."

Jay didn't reply.

"You don't have to be defensive," he said at last. "Nobody is judging you for killing in self defense...except for you."

Elle blinked back tears. All her life, she had been the quiet child, the demure one. And now she was a hardened survivor, a girl who killed Klan members when she had to. She hated killing. Despised it.

But in this world, her options were slim.

Option A: Be killed.

Option B: Kill.

As soon as they were a couple of miles away from the Pits, they slowed their jog to a fast walk. There had been no sign of Georgia and Pix yet, and Flash was panicking. Elle told him to relax. They were going to be at the bakery – that was the plan, and Elle had seen Georgia and Pix escape during the chaos. They would be there.

It would be okay.

"So what *were* you?" Jay asked, adjusting his jacket.

"What *was* I?" Elle asked.

"Before everything happened. What were you?"

"I was just like everybody else," she said. "I was just a kid."

"But where are you from? Did you live in L.A. before…well, everything?"

"Beverly Hills," Elle answered. "I was a freshman. Would have been a sophomore this year." She sighed. "Too bad. I had plans."

Jay grunted. "Tell me about it," he murmured.

Elle saw Georgia out of the corner of her eye. Her long, thin frame was pressed against the brick siding of a building. Pix was clinging to her arm. They both looked terrified.

"Georgia," Elle stated, nodding in her direction.

Flash surged forward, toward his sister. They embraced.

"You made it," Pix said.

Georgia hugged Jay. He squeezed her back, and Elle wondered what it would be like to be hugged like that.

"Elle," Georgia panted, "I'm sorry. I lost you in the rush, but I had to get Pix out of there."

Elle shrugged it off. She felt awkward, watching everyone else embrace.

"Let's get back to the bakery," Elle said. "The Klan will be looking for us. Especially me."

"Elle," Pix whispered, tugging on her sleeve. "Thank you for coming for me."

Elle cleared her throat. She wasn't used to gratitude.

"Come on, let's move," she mumbled.

They followed her through the darkness. They didn't speak until sunrise, when they reached the bakery. They pushed inside, exhausted. Elle collapsed on the floor, her back against the counter.

"I thought we'd never make it," Georgia sighed, lying flat on her back. "God, what we just did was insane."

"You should get out of the city," Elle advised. "The Klan will look for you. And once they start hunting someone, they don't stop. Ever."

"You would know, wouldn't you?" Jay replied. "They've been hunting you for a long time, haven't they? You were a fighter in the Pits. That's why you know so much about the Klan, and that's how you knew where to find Pix."

Elle slid her backpack off her shoulders. She was dead tired.

"Yeah," she admitted. "I was a prisoner in the Pits."

"And you escaped."

The ghost of a smile tugged at the corner of Elle's mouth.

"Yes," she said.

"How did you do it?"

Elle drew a circle in the dust on the floor.

"I just waited for the right moment," she answered. "The Klan is dangerous, but not all of them are smart. In fact, a lot of them are pretty stupid." She pulled the sleeve of her jacket down. Her shoulder was black and blue, bruised. "Ouch."

"Tomas did that to you," Jay stated. "That looks painful."

"It's not bad."

"How long were you in the Pits?"

Elle shook her head.

"I don't know. Two months, maybe?" She shrugged. "It wasn't that long after Day Zero. I came to the city, hoping to find my family. I got caught by the Klan instead. I've been here ever since."

"If the Klan is hunting you," Flash said carefully, "why don't you leave the city?"

"Because I don't know what's out there," Elle replied.

Jay and Georgia shared a secretive glance.

"What?" Elle demanded.

"In the bunker," Jay answered, his tone even, "we had a radio. A ham radio. We had contact with some people before we left."

"You had radio contact with other survivors?" Elle asked, bewildered.

"Yes. And militia groups. That's how we kept track of what was happening in the outside world," Georgia said. "The only reason we left the bunker was because we ran out of food and water."

"Elle, you should leave the city," Jay interjected. "Staying here is suicide."

"Leaving is suicide. Omega is almost everywhere," Elle pointed out.

"Sacramento is safe," Pix said. She straightened her spine. "We heard it on the radio. That's where we're going. We're trying to get there."

"Sacramento is a long way from here, sunshine," Elle deadpanned.

"It's a National Guard stronghold," Jay replied. "And the California militias are cleaning up the Central Valley. Omega isn't *everywhere*, Elle. We came to Hollywood because we thought we might be able to scavenge for some supplies, but we're not staying. We're heading out. To safety."

Elle looked at the four of them. They were really into this idea.

"How do you know this isn't some kind of a trap to lure survivors into Sacramento?" Elle asked, raising her eyebrows. "At the beginning, right after Day Zero, Omega set up emergency relief camps. It was a big trap. They brought people in just so they could kill them."

She knew because Uncle had told her. Uncle had *seen* it.

"This isn't Omega," Georgia answered, firm. "This is safe."

"Nothing is safe."

"Well, it's either Sacramento or *this*," Jay retorted. He took the handgun from his belt and held it in front of Elle's face. "Is this fun, Elle? Do you like having to shoot people?"

His voice was harsh, and Elle recoiled.

"You don't know what it's like to survive out here," she snapped. "It's getting worse every day."

"So take a chance and come with us to Sacramento," Georgia said. "You're smart and you know more about survival than any of us. We could all help each other – and you wouldn't be alone anymore. We'd be a big, happy family." Georgia winked. "You know you want to, shortstack."

Elle hesitated. The idea was appealing. Being alone was the *smart* thing…but being with people, with *friends*…that would be nice. Very nice.

"Leaving means admitting that my mother is dead," Elle said.

Jay said nothing for a long time before reaching over and touching Elle's hand. She stiffened at the warmth of his fingers. He smiled softly.

"We're all orphans," he said. "We all have a common goal. We all need to survive. Juvenile delinquents or not."

Elle pushed the hair away from her face.

The Klan would hunt for her. They would never stop, and eventually, they would find her. And then they would kill her, and that would be the end of everything. Leaving the city was a terrifying prospect, but it also brought about the hope of a safe haven. What if there really was something out there...something *safe*?

Something sparked in Elle's chest.

Hope.

"If I come with you," Elle said, choosing her words with caution, "you have to listen to me. You're all clumsy and noisy. You'll get us killed in a couple of days. You have to be willing to take advice."

To her surprise, Jay started laughing.

"I think we figured that out, Elle," he chuckled. "Don't worry. We'll listen to your tips and tricks. They've worked so far."

Elle was pleased with his answer.

"Before we go to Sacramento, there's somewhere we need to go first," she said. "My Aunt and Uncle, they had a home in the Tehachapi Mountains. I left it to come back to the city to search for my family. If they're still there, they'll be able to help us get to Sacramento."

"You have living family members?" Flash asked. He tilted his head. "Lucky."

Elle wasn't so sure. She didn't even know if Aunt and Uncle were still alive.

"We go there first, and then we go north," Elle stated. "What do you say?"

Georgia reached for a cigarette – she seemed to have an endless supply.

"Sounds good to me," she said.

"I'm in," Jay added.

Pix and Flash raised their hands.

Elle nodded. She would go with them to Sacramento, and if they betrayed her, she would leave. It was a simple plan. Either way, she was escaping the Klan. She was escaping the memory of a dead family. She was escaping Day Zero.

Chapter Nine

"Do **not** do this, Elle," Aunt said.

Her pretty white hair was mussed. It was the middle of the night, and Elle was standing at the doorway, her backpack over her shoulder. The night was cold and brisk.

"I have to!" Elle replied. "I can't just stay here. Maybe she's still alive."

"Your mother is dead," Aunt answered, her voice firm. Almost cold. "If you go back, all you'll find is an empty apartment."

"I have to try. She would come looking for me if it were the other way around." Elle shook her head. "Explain it to Uncle. He'll be mad at first, but he'll understand."

"He's seen the city. He knows what it's like."

"I know."

"The city is death."

Elle flinched. Her mother had said that very thing to her not so long ago.

"I'm sorry," Elle said, fighting tears. "I have to go."

Aunt folded her arms across her chest. She wasn't going to hug Elle, and she wasn't going to cry. Aunt was too hardened for that – too much like Elle.

"I'll be back," Elle promised.

Aunt said nothing. She didn't believe her.

"Goodbye," Elle whispered.

She stepped over the threshold.

She left the safety of Aunt and Uncle's home behind.

"I had a six-month sentence," Georgia said.

It was mid-afternoon, and they were inside Elle's apartment, gathering every last scrap of food and supplies she had here. It had taken everything in Elle to show them where she lived – show them her dismal stash of supplies. But now that she was leaving…well, she needed all the supplies she could get her hands on.

They couldn't go back to the underground basement and scavenge food.

The Klan had taken it.

"What did you do?" Elle asked.

"I sold drugs for my older brother. You know. I was all cute and innocent-looking-" she batted her eyelashes with dramatic flare "- and he'd send me outside to do the exchanges. I got wise, and I started selling my own drugs on the side."

"And then you got arrested, which wasn't so wise," Elle remarked.

"Yeah." A shadow fell across Georgia's face. "It was a mistake. All of it was." She sighed. "I grew up in Atlanta. It's a nice city, you know? A couple years ago my mom moved to California with her new boyfriend, and that's when things got real bad."

Elle opened the cupboards in the kitchen.

"We all make mistakes," she said. "Welcome to the human race."

"Well..." Georgia gave Elle a sly look, gesturing to Flash and Pix on the other side of the apartment, going through their own packs. "Those two were in juvie for credit card hacking. Like, *major* hacking."

"That explains the nicknames," Elle commented. "They don't really seem like the criminal types, though."

"They're not. Their foster parents were using their brilliant little minds to hack bank accounts and everything else." Georgia smirked. "Ironic thing is, Pix and Flash ended up in the correctional facility, but the foster parents didn't get any time. They got off without anything."

"That's stupid."

"That's the justice system, sweet pea. Everything was blamed on the twins."

Elle rolled her eyes.

"Like I said," she sighed. "Welcome to the human race."

She peeked over her shoulder at Jay, who was gathering Elle's stash of ammunition from the closet. "What's Jay's story?" Elle whispered.

Georgia picked up a can of peaches and studied the label.

"Wish I knew," she shrugged. "He won't tell."

"He's keeping secrets?" Elle zipped her backpack shut, doing a final sweep of the supplies in the kitchen. "How bad do you think he was?"

"I don't know." Georgia threw the peach can into her own pack. "The thing is, most of the kids in juvie weren't bad, they were just...*lost*. Like me. We didn't mean to get off track, we just didn't have anybody there to tell us we were doing the wrong thing." An expression of profound sadness spread across her face. "It took the end of the world to change us."

Elle bit her lip.

"The end changed everybody," she whispered.

Jay slammed a duffel bag on the counter.

"That," he announced, "is a freaking huge bag of ammunition for a girl your size. Where did you *get* all of this?"

"I've been collecting it," Elle replied. "We don't have much food, but we'll have plenty of ammunition."

"For two guns," Georgia chuckled. "That's overkill."

"If you've got something good, don't waste it," Elle said. "Ammunition and food are the two most important things we could bring with us. The ammo goes. The blankets stay."

"But it's cold out there, Elle," Pix complained.

"Trust me, you're better off with more bullets than blankets," Elle assured her. "There are bad people out there – people worse than the Klan. We want to be able to protect ourselves."

"What about this bag?" Georgia asked.

"We'll divide the ammo up between our packs," Elle said. "And then the rest of it can stay in the duffel bag. Jay, you can carry it because you're the strongest."

Jay rolled his eyes.

"Right, stereotype the big guy."

"Hey, it's not my fault that you're the oldest and the strongest," Elle said. "We'll all have an equal load to carry, believe me."

It took just under an hour to finish packing. Pix, Flash and Georgia were each loaded with a backpack. Jay carried a bigger pack and the biggest duffel bag filled with Elle's salvaged ammunition. Elle had already assembled her pack. It contained all of the necessary items: Water, purifying tablets, knives, matches, bandages and alcohol for cleaning open wounds, along with needles and thread.

"So." Georgia blinked. "Are we ready? Can we go?"

Elle looked at the apartment and the view of the Santa Monica Beach. Sadness squeezed her heart like an icy fist. She would probably never come back to this place. She would be separated from the city that reminded her of her family for the rest of her life.

"Yeah," she said. "We can go."

Flash and Pix were the first out the door, followed by Georgia. Jay lingered for a moment.

"It's going to be okay," he told her.

Elle met his gaze.

"Yeah," she replied.

Elle walked out of the apartment last, shutting the door behind her. She climbed down the dark, dusty staircase, and met the others on Ocean Boulevard below. The salty sea breeze rustled her hair. She looked up at the city.

This time, she was saying goodbye for good.

Elle had carefully charted out their route in her mind. They would parallel the 405 Interstate, the San Diego Freeway, out of the city. They would merge onto Interstate 5, heading northbound. And then they would find themselves in the Tehachapi Hills, at Aunt and Uncle's house.

"So, are your Aunt and Uncle friendly?" Georgia asked.

Elle shrugged. "If they're still there, yeah."

"Where exactly do they live?"

"The Tehachapi Hills. They have a ranch."

"You left the safety of a ranch hidden in the mountains to go back to the city and look for your family?" Jay asked. "Why?"

Elle made a face.

Why did he *think*?

"So you think they'll have food and supplies?" Jay continued, pretending he'd never asked a stupid question.

"That's right," Elle replied.

"Are you sure it's safe?"

"Nothing is safe, anymore. Or haven't you noticed?" Elle sighed. "My aunt and uncle will be able to help us."

"That's *awesome*," Flash remarked, looking up. "Hey. If their ranch is safe, why don't we just stay there with them?"

Elle shook her head.

"No. They're...involved with the military. With the militias that are fighting Omega. It's too high risk."

"Oh." Flash looked crushed. Pix squeezed his shoulder.

"Why didn't you just go back to live with your aunt and uncle after you escaped the Pits?" Pix asked. "Why did you choose to stay in the city?"

"I was hoping," Elle whispered. "And I guess I was afraid to leave."

"Hoping for what?"

Elle didn't answer. She had been *hoping* that she would find her mother at some point. That she wasn't dead. Elle had stayed in the city because it was her connection to the past – the world before Day Zero.

Now she was leaving, and she would put it behind her. All of it.

"So this is the freeway." Georgia stared at the crumbling remains of a decrepit overpass. "Are you sure it's okay to follow this out of the city?"

"Of course it's not okay," Elle snorted. "But we don't really have any other choice. I don't want to get lost, so we're going to parallel the road."

"What if there are bandits or something on the highway?"

"We're very well armed," Elle said with confidence she didn't feel. "Come on. We need to start before it gets too dark. The Klan comes out at night, and Omega patrols certain parts of the city during the day."

They climbed the onramp to the freeway. A Chinese restaurant adjacent to the highway had been blown apart. They stepped onto the freeway itself. Miles of vehicles stretched as far as the eye could see.

"It looks like a river of metal," Pix commented.

"None of them work anymore?" Georgia sighed.

"Not if they had an electronic ignition," Pix explained, brightening. "See, an electromagnetic pulse disables anything that functions with a computer chip. A pulse bomb can come from anything – a nuclear bomb detonated in the atmosphere, or even a solar flare."

"This was no solar flare," Elle said sharply. "This was an attack."

Her words hung in the air for a moment.

"Yeah," Pix said at last. "It wasn't an accident."

They walked. In some places, the cars were so tightly packed together that they had to climb on hoods and roofs to get through. There were remnants of a past civilization inside the vehicles – cracked, broken cellphones, GPS devices and MP3 players.

Georgia peeked through the window of a blue hatchback. She stifled a gasp and jumped backward.

"There's a dead person in the car!" Georgia said.

"Keep it down, will you?" Elle snapped. "Your voice is echoing."

"But there's-"

"-I know, I know." Elle gave her shoulder a brief squeeze. "Keep a sharp lookout, okay?"

Georgia turned to Jay and he murmured something to her – probably words of comfort. Elle wanted to roll her eyes, but she didn't. These kids hadn't seen half of the things Day Zero had dished out. They were still getting used to the dead bodies.

They'd learn soon enough.

As they trudged forward, Georgia kept her gaze straight ahead, refusing to look through the windows of any of the vehicles on the road. She had gone pale. Elle remembered when she was like that.

Georgia would harden.

They all would.

"I had a whole network built," Georgia explained, grinning devilishly. They were camped on the side of a foothill, tucked away in a crevice, out of sight of the road. Elle and the others warmed their hands in front of a small fire they had built.

"What kind of a network?" Elle asked.

"Business connections," Georgia replied. "My brother had a hefty stash of drugs, and he was high half the time, so I'd swipe them and sell them to my own customers. It was great. I always had cash in my pocket."

"Right. It was great until you went to *jail*," Pix smirked.

"You should talk, you little hacker," Georgia shot back.

"At least I wasn't selling dope to thugs on the street in Los Angeles."

"Hey, calm down," Jay interjected, hiding a smile. "We all made mistakes, and it's over now. What we did back then was in the past. This is the apocalypse, remember?"

"What happened to your brother?" Elle asked Georgia.

"Don't know," Georgia sniffed. "He was a half-baked lunatic any way you slice it. I'm guessing he died when everything collapsed. I wouldn't know. I was in *prison* when it all went down."

She acted nonchalant, but Elle could hear the emotion in Georgia's voice.

"What about you, Jay?" Elle asked, the flames throwing shadows over her face.

Jay held his hands in front of the fire.

"Doesn't matter," he shrugged.

"Come on. We've all confessed," Georgia prodded. "You can, too. We're not going to tell anybody. I mean, there's ain't anybody left to tell, anyway."

Jay just shook his head.

"Not every story's worth telling," he murmured, looking down.

Hmm. Elle knew how *that* worked.

"We should all get some sleep," she said. "You guys go ahead. I'll take the first watch. Jay, you want to take the second watch?"

"Sure."

They kept the fire burning as they curled up and went to sleep. Elle stationed herself above the campsite, huddled in the darkness. She pulled her hood around her face and scanned the horizon. The freeway wound around the curve of the mountain. If they traveled fast, they could reach the ranch in three days.

If they could stay alive long enough, that is.

Chapter Ten

As they followed the 405, they bypassed abandoned rest stops and gas stations. Elle warned the kids not to stop at any of the buildings. Oftentimes roadside stops had become traps for wandering travelers. It was a great way to get robbed and killed.

Neither of which were appealing. At all.

"Here we go," Elle announced, pointing to an off ramp. "We follow this road and by this time tomorrow, we'll be there!"

She was excited. Aunt and Uncle would be so surprised to see her. They probably thought she was dead. She had disappeared such a long time ago...what if they had forgotten about her?

No, Elle thought. *They would never forget about me...right?*

Elle was far more comfortable as soon as they left the freeway. The road that they were following was older, and as they progressed, became smaller. It was hardly ever traveled, and the lack of tire tracks made it obvious that there had been no recent traffic in this area.

To Elle, that meant just one thing: Omega hadn't been here.

Yet.

They pushed on, walking until their feet hurt. The open space of the mountains was a huge change from the snug confines of the city. Elle felt exposed, like she was walking around with a huge target on her back that said: SHOOT ME. It put her on edge, but the fresh air and the stunning scenery was terrific.

"I almost forgot what it was like to have this much space around me," Elle commented. "I'm so used to Hollywood and Santa Monica. Everything is squished together there."

"It's a good change," Jay replied. "There's freedom out here."

Yeah. Maybe he was right.

They traveled all day, making camp at nightfall. Elle wrapped her hands in strips of cloth to keep them warm, pulling her hood around her face. She leaned her head against her backpack. The earth was slightly damp, leaving streaks of dirt on her pants. Jay made a small fire when it got dark, enough to warm the kids' pinched, red faces.

Sleeping in the wide-open spaces was different than sleeping within the confines of an apartment building. The sky was dark, deep blue. Elle stared at the stars. The longer she watched them, the more she seemed to see. She fell asleep, sucked into the mesmerizing swirl of the Milky Way.

Early morning came too quickly. It was bitterly cold. Elle sat up, flexing her stiff fingers. She nudged the others awake. They moved slowly, shivering in the frigid temperature. The remains of the fire smoldered in the coolness of the morning. Jay stamped it out with his boots, hiding traces of their presence.

"Breakfast," Elle muttered, opening her backpack.

She took two sealed granola bars and split them between the five kids. It wasn't appetizing, but it was heavy enough to tame the hunger pains. For now.

They left the campsite.

As they followed the road, they wound upward around wide, dry hills. Drought-resistant foliage was clumped together in places and patches of forest lined the mountaintops. They stopped once to eat a snack and drink water, then kept moving again. They didn't want to stop. Stopping was dangerous. Constant movement gave them a better chance of survival – this was something Elle had learned the hard way, after months of living in the city, being hunted by bloodthirsty Klan members.

In late evening, they finally arrived.

"We're here!" Elle said.

She jogged forward, up the last part of the road. It flattened into a gravel driveway. The driveway led to a ranch house. It was painted in muted tones, blending with the hills. The house was surrounded by a chain link fence.

"Nice place," Georgia remarked. "Were your folks rich?"

"My parents weren't rich," Elle corrected. "But my Aunt and Uncle were."

"What did they do?"

"My Aunt's family was cattle ranchers…probably a hundred years ago."

"Ah. Lots of money," Jay muttered.

As Elle approached the chain link fence, she noticed that it was hanging open. She stared at the front door. Weeds were growing around the entrance steps.

"The dogs are gone," she whispered.

"The dogs?" Pix echoed.

"There were German Shepherds. Lots of them."

Elle pushed the gate open and whistled softly. There was no answer, no barking. She followed the path to the front door and jiggled the handle. It was unlocked. She pushed the door open and gripped the handgun tucked into her belt.

"Elle...this is wrong, isn't it?" Flash said, his voice shaking.

"Very wrong," Elle replied.

The door swung open and revealed a long hallway. The spacious rooms were empty. Curtains were drawn.

"They're gone," she breathed. A sob lodged in her throat. "They haven't been here for a long time."

"What do you think happened?" Georgia asked.

"I don't know."

Elle walked to the end of the hall, turning into the living room – a familiar spot for her. The couches and chairs had been covered with white sheets. Dim sunlight filtered through the slits in the shuttered windows. The house was cold, empty. Elle stared at a mirror hanging above the empty fireplace.

She was alone. Again.

Elle huddled against the back of the cage, panting. She was caked in filth. The Klan had taken a knife to her thick black hair and hacked it off. Blood slipped down the back of her neck. She'd never been so dirty before. She'd never been so tired.

She'd just witnessed a fight in the Pits. Two women, both middle aged, thrown into a muddy, deep pit. Thrown against each other in a fight for their lives.

A fight to the death, the Klan called it. But Elle couldn't do it. She couldn't kill her opponents. They were prisoners, just like her. Forced into a sick, twisted game used as a form of entertainment.

Sooner or later, she would end up dead, too.

Someone would kill her, out of desperation.

The night was cold. She shuddered and watched the Klan guards round the park, lighting the torches. Tomas stood near the bonfire in the center of the rows of cages, warming his hands. His tattoos and the shadows from the flames became one in the dim lighting. Elle hated the sight of him. He was a sadist – the embodiment of everything Day Zero had done to the world.

Tomas felt Elle's gaze on him and he turned, offering a smug smile.

She buried her head in her knees, hiding her face.

There had to be a way out of this hell, she thought. There was always a way.

She peeked through the bars and looked at the cages, at the guards making their normal rounds. There was a routine here, a rhythm of operation – even if the Klan was little more than an oversized group of organized thugs.

Elle drew a square in the dirt.

That was the beginning of her map.

Aunt and Uncle's rooms were abandoned. Everything important had been stripped and taken from the house. Elle found traces of broken glass and splintered wood in the corners of the rooms. Something had happened. Aunt and Uncle had left suddenly, but someone else had cleaned the house up after their departure.

Who?

It was dark. Elle sat in the large, rustic kitchen.

"Where would they have gone?" Georgia asked.

She sat near Pix and Flash on the countertop, biting off a piece of jerky. Jay sat next to Elle.

"I don't know," Elle shrugged. "The only reason they would have left would be if Omega found them. They were working with the National Guard and the militias that are fighting Omega – it was dangerous work. Anything could have happened."

"But where would they go if they were...well, still alive?" Georgia continued. "They must have had a backup plan that you knew about, right?"

"Not really," Elle answered. "I only lived here for a few weeks. They were just starting to help the militias when I left."

"Well," Jay spoke up, breaking the depressing conversation, "I guess there's only one thing we can do: keep heading toward Sacramento."

"It's hundreds of miles from here," Georgia sighed.

"It's safe," Pix whispered.

"Oh, I know. I'm just saying." Georgia kicked her boots up on the counter. "It could take us weeks to get there."

"We don't have a choice," Jay replied. "We've got to keep moving. If Omega knows where this house is, they might be watching it. It's not safe to stay here."

"He's right," Elle agreed. "We should get out of here as soon as possible."

"Are there any old cars that we could use here?" Flash asked.

"I don't know. We could look." Elle jumped off the counter. "My Aunt used to keep horses in the stables behind the house, but they're empty now. I don't know what happened to the animals."

She opened the kitchen door. It led to the backyard. Moonlight fell across the overgrown gardens and the dry fountain. Elle bypassed the stables and approached an old shed.

"Aunt and Uncle were smart," Elle said. "They didn't keep their stuff out in the open, where people could steal it."

"They hid it in the shed?" Georgia asked. "That's so original."

Elle smirked.

She opened the shed door. It was a fancy building with high-beamed ceilings. It smelled like must and rust. Elle hadn't been here for a long time. She'd only come inside once, when Uncle had shown her the shed, in case of an emergency...

She flicked the light switch for the heck of it. Nothing happened.

Elle pulled back the thick curtain over the window near the worktable, shedding moonlight inside the building.

She walked to the far corner, counting her steps.

"Help me move this-" she began, but Georgia cut her off.

"Oh, my god!"

"What?" Elle demanded.

"Look!"

Georgia pointed. Elle's eyes adjusted to the darkness and she could see Jay climbing on something. It was a car of some sort.

"What is it?" Elle asked.

She knew a lot about the Klan and Hollywood, but she didn't know anything about cars.

"It's a Suzuki Samurai," Jay beamed, patting the hood.

Georgia and Elle shared a confused glance. They got closer to the car. It was a jeep. There was no roof, just four seats. It was painted a muted tan tone.

"It's a jeep," Elle stated.

"It's not just a jeep," Jay corrected. "This, ladies and gentlemen, is an EMP-proof 1989 Suzuki Samurai."

Realization dawned on the twins.

"It doesn't have an electronic chip," they said at the same time.

"Which means the EMP didn't affect it," Georgia added.

"And it's been inside a big metal shed," Pix pointed out. "Just like a faraday cage."

"That's awesome," Elle agreed. "But now if I could get someone to *help* me, I'll show you something that will make you all really happy."

"We don't have the keys for the jeep, anyway," Georgia sighed. "We couldn't start it to even see if there's gas in the tank."

"And we have no gas," Pix added.

"Not true," Jay replied. "I can hotwire this thing – I don't need keys."

"Hey, you *guys*!" Elle said, crossing her arms. "Would you listen to me for two seconds? Help me move this worktable."

Jay, Georgia and the twins each took a side of the table and pulled it forward, away from the window.

"Geez, thanks," Elle said, rolling her eyes. "Took long enough."

A multi-colored rug had been rolled out under the table. Elle pulled it up, revealing a hidden door. Elle tapped it with the toe of her shoe.

"Ta-da," she said. "A secret storeroom. Emergency fuel. You're welcome."

Georgia whooped loudly.

"YES!" she said. "We don't have to walk all the way to Sacramento!"

Jay laughed aloud.

"Finally," he said. "A stroke of good luck."

Chapter Eleven

Elle had waited a long time for this. She curled her fingers around the bars on the cage, looking around the park. It was nearly sundown. She sat back down on the floor, staring at the map she had drawn in the dirt. It had taken her weeks to create it, but she had finally constructed a decent replication of the layout of the park. Every cage, every pit, every guarded Klan hotspot.

She had tucked a knife into her boot. She'd stolen it earlier from Tomas when he had been sleeping, hung over. He had so many knives and weapons hanging off his belt.

Your loss, my gain, Elle thought bitterly.

As soon as it was dark, she would use the knife to work through the wire holding the cyclone cage closed. And then she would navigate the park, slip out of the boundaries of Klan territory...and she would be free.

She hoped she survived.

The jeep was running. Jay had hotwired the thing, and it was rumbling. It had been so long since Elle had heard the sound of an engine. Outside of Omega's Humvees and patrol vehicles, there were no more cars.

The kids had found a small trailer in the shed and hooked it to the hitch on the back of the jeep. They had filled the trailer with gas canisters. The few supplies that they had scavenged in the city remained in their backpacks.

The jeep itself was only built to hold four people, but Pix and Flash were small, and they were able to cram three people in the backseat instead of two. Elle crawled into the front passenger seat, next to Jay, who sat behind the wheel. He was happy to be in control of the vehicle.

"So were you a car thief?" Elle inquired slyly.

Jay only grinned. "Why do you say that?"

"You seem to be an expert in hotwiring cars."

Jay laughed, his white teeth a flash against the early morning darkness.

"I'm not an expert," he replied. "I'm just...I have a wide range of skills, let's put it that way."

Elle wasn't buying it. She plopped her backpack down at her feet. Georgia, Pix and Flash hopped into the backseat. The trailer was secured and they had enough gas to get them to Sacramento. They shouldn't have a problem.

The thought excited Elle.

"I haven't been in a car in ages," Georgia drawled, chewing on a piece of gum. "Not since I was arrested, and the ride in the back of the cop car *sucked*."

"That's what you get for being a criminal," Elle commented.

Georgia stuck her tongue out at Elle, and she laughed.

"The engine seems to be in good condition," Flash said, adopting his teacher voice. "Pix and I haven't found any problems with it, other than the fact that the battery is low."

"Thank you, Professor," Georgia replied, making a face. "Can you *please* can the child-genius comments for just an hour. *Please*?"

Flash folded his arms across his chest, insulted. Pix patted his shoulder.

They couldn't help being smart. They just were.

"Are we ready?" Elle asked, looking over her shoulder.

"Yes," Georgia answered. "But I want to know why you get to sit in the front. I'm one of the oldest ones here."

"How do you know *I'm* not the oldest one here?" Elle pointed out.

Georgia blew a bubble.

"Oh? How old *are* you, Tinkerbell?"

"Fifteen and a half."

"Ha. I'm seventeen. You're a mere child."

Elle rolled her eyes.

"Let's just go, okay?" Jay sighed. "Everybody in? Good. Say goodbye to the ranch."

He slowly shifted gears and pulled away from the house. The gravel driveway crunched under the Suzuki's tires. Elle refused to look at the ranch house. She just watched the shadow of the building fade into the rearview mirror as Jay eased the jeep and the trailer down the mountain road.

She hoped her Aunt and Uncle were safe, wherever they were.

She hoped Sacramento was all that they hoped it would be.

She hoped that they would all survive this road trip.

Chapter Twelve

Elle knelt next to Pix, touching her forehead. The girl's skin was on fire. Her face was drained of color and her breathing was heavy, labored. It was raining. Everyone was cold and wet. Flash's face was pinched. He held his glasses in his hand, teary-eyed. Georgia was standing next to the jeep, taking a nervous drag on a cigarette. The girl was rattled.

"What do we do?" Flash whispered.

Pix was lying across the backseat, semiconscious. She had been sick for two days, and it had slowed down their progress. They were stopped on the side of the road, past Bakersfield, California, near the Kern River. Interstate 5 stretched north and south as far as the eye could see, paralleling the golden coastal mountains on one side and the Central Valley on the other.

"We've got to get her medicine," Jay said. His fingers curled into fists. "She's dying."

"We don't have medicine," Flash said, choked up. "We've got nothing."

Elle continued to hold Pix's limp, sweaty hand.

Georgia was silent, wordless. She was angry that their journey to Sacramento, to safe haven, had been stopped by something as seemingly petty as Flash being sick.

Elle wished she'd grow up. Everyone wanted to get to Sacramento.

If Pix was sick, that wasn't her fault.

"We're close to a rest stop," Elle pointed out. She had spent a lot of time studying the maps from Aunt and Uncle's ranch house. "There's a community a few miles from here, and there's probably a pharmacy in town. We can search it and look for something that might help her."

"I thought we were supposed to *avoid* towns," Georgia snapped.

"We were," Jay replied, his tone sharp. "But Pix's sick. We don't have a choice."

Georgia closed her mouth, throwing her cigarette to the ground.

"Jay and I will go into town," Elle said. "Georgia, you stay with Pix and Flash. Keep them safe."

How did this happen? Just two days ago, they had left the ranch house in the Tehachapi hills full of high hopes. They had a car, gas, supplies and a map. They were on their way to Sacramento, the rumored safe haven for wartime survivors and militia fighters.

Nothing ever went as planned.

2 Days Earlier

Elle could smell the blood. Georgia leaned over the side of the Suzuki and puked. Pix and Flash gripped the door handles tightly. Jay stopped the jeep and they sat there, staring at the huge expanse of freeway that curved down the last stretch of the Tehachapi hills – the Grapevine.

Parts of the highway had been blown apart. Chunks of concrete was scattered throughout the hills. Dead bodies were strewn through patches of dry grass. The air stank of rotting flesh and there were spots in the soil where the rain had mixed with blood, creating red rivers in the mud.

"What happened here?" Georgia breathed, shaking.

Elle closed her eyes, took a deep breath, and looked at the scene again.

"This was a battle," she said. "Omega versus somebody else."

"Who was the 'somebody else?'" Jay said.

"Us," Pix replied automatically. "Look at the dead. They're Omega. They're mostly Chinese, too. I see some National Guard uniforms out there, though."

"So this was a fight between the National Guard and Omega," Jay said. "Unbelievable. They just left the dead here to rot?"

"This was pretty recent," Flash observed.

"Should we go back?" Pix asked.

"No. There's nothing for us down south," Jay replied.

"We can't drive on the road the whole way. So much of it has been blown to pieces."

"We'll use the side roads."

"I don't see any signs of Omega," Georgia added. "And I don't see any signs of the United States military, either."

Elle's heart sank.

She had been hoping that they would run across the United States military, somehow, and that they would be protected. Surely the National Guard would take care of survivors. That's why they were going to Sacramento, after all.

But that wasn't happening. Not today.

"We need to get out of here," Elle said. "They could come back."

"This battle is over," Jay replied, clenching his fist. "We have to keep going."

No one argued. They didn't want to go back to the city, and the only way to escape was to keep heading north. So they did. Jay navigated side roads, trying to keep the trailer from getting rocked too much. The gasoline was too valuable to lose.

It took hours to get down the mountain.

Elle tried to avoid looking at the dead that hadn't been collected from the battlefield. Many of them had been blown to pieces. She'd never seen anything so horrible.

"Do you think it's like this everywhere?" Pix whispered.

Elle didn't answer. She hoped it wasn't.

By the time they reached the bottom of the mountain, night had fallen. They passed a rest stop, Laval Road. Signs of recent military presence were everywhere. An American flag had been painted across a freeway overpass. Someone had scrawled USA FOREVER on the side of an abandoned restaurant.

"USA forever," Georgia snorted. "Wishful thinking."

"At least someone's trying to keep hope alive," Elle replied.

"It doesn't do anything." Georgia watched the scenery roll by, a blank expression on her face. "We're dead. The United States, everything good about it. It's gone. And it's not coming back."

Elle sighed. It was easy to believe that. Very easy.

The question was...was *she* going to believe it?

Jay rolled onto a freeway ramp that veered left, keeping onto the Interstate 5 freeway. It would take them straight to Sacramento if they weren't stopped by Omega patrols. *That,* of course, was the trick. None of them knew where Omega was coming from or where they were keeping their forces. If they stumbled across an armed force of soldiers...

Well. It would be bad.

They drove until it was too dark to see the road. Jay decided that using the lights on the jeep would be too risky – they could be spotted a mile away – so they voted against traveling at night. They pulled over to a sheltered area on the side of the road, unrolled a piece of canvas over the roof and hunkered down for a dinner of cold canned food and stale crackers.

And then they slept.

"Pix's missing!"

Flash was panicking. He circled the jeep twice, the color drained from his face. Elle sat up, grabbing the door handle. She had fallen asleep slumped across Jay's knees. Realizing this, the blood rushed to her cheeks. She hoped he hadn't noticed.

Jay was wide-awake already, jumping out of the jeep.

Good. He hadn't.

"Missing?" Georgia practically screeched. "*Again?* How many times is she going to do this to us?"

Elle climbed out of the jeep, onto the gravel. They were parked behind an overgrown bush on the side of the freeway. It was cold – low thirties. She shivered and looked around. Flash was right; there was no sign of Pix.

"Why would she wander off?" Jay said, and Elle could see that he was angry. "What's wrong with her?"

"Maybe she just had to pee," Georgia suggested. "She might be right back."

"No. I've been calling and calling for her," Flash replied, adjusting his glasses.

"She must have gotten turned around," Jay said.

Georgia gestured to the sprawling, flat landscape around them.

"How could you get lost here?" she demanded. "It's impossible!"

"Anything is possible," Elle said. "The grass is high and there are lots of shadows. Jay's right...she must have gotten lost when she got up. When did you notice she was gone, Flash?"

"Just now – I woke up and she wasn't next to me."

He seemed embarrassed that he had managed to sleep through his sister's disappearance.

Jay answered, "We need to find her. She doesn't have any food or water with her. She'll get dehydrated fast."

"Let's split up," Georgia suggested, sighing. "We'll be able to find her faster."

Jay pulled the map out of the side door of the jeep and spread it flat against the hood. He pulled a pen out of his pocket and marked their location with a small X. "We don't go more than two miles away from this spot," he said. "We'll meet here in two hours."

Elle looked at the map. Georgia was right – it would be difficult to get lost with the miles of flat freeway and grassy plains on each side of them. It would take hours to reach the top of the coastal hills on their left...and Pix hadn't been gone that long. Besides, why would she wander that far in the first place?

She wouldn't. Not if she was in her right mind, anyway.

No, something was wrong.

They each headed in a different direction. Elle liked being alone, separated from the rest. It gave her time to think, to get in touch with her surroundings on a different level. She'd hardly had a moment of silence since she'd joined the group.

Silence was something she missed.

She walked through the tall, golden grass until the jeep and the bush were specks in the distance. The grass was taller than her in most places, and Elle realized that it would be easy for Pix – who was short – to get lost here. She quietly called her name but received no reply.

I can't believe it, Elle thought. *Why am I even here? Wasting my time, looking for a kid that doesn't even have enough common sense to stay in the stupid jeep while we're all sleeping...*

Elle tried to put the anger out of her mind, but it was still there, simmering under the surface. For the second time, she was sticking her neck out for Pix – for this group of kids. And for what reason? They hadn't done anything for her. So far, she'd been the one who had helped *them* stay alive.

Stop overthinking, she thought. *Just look for Pix.*

An hour passed. Elle searched through every stretch of tall grass that she could find, calling Pix's name. She came up short, checking the time.

Where *was* she?

At the hour and a half mark, Elle turned around and started heading back to the jeep. She hoped someone else had found Pix. If not, they would be stuck in this godforsaken strip of wilderness forever. She hopped across a dry creek carved into the terrain, shielded by tufts of six-foot tall grass.

Elle stopped and bent down. What looked like a pile of discolored rags was crammed on the side of the creek. She tilted her head. It was an odd shape. She got closer, realization dawning.

"Pix?"

She splashed through the shallow creek bed and grabbed the pile. It *was* Pix, and she was unconscious. Her little face was slack. Elle checked her pulse. Pix's heart was still beating. But why was she unconscious?

She bundled the girl in her arms and struggled up the creek bed, through the grass. Pix was small, but so was Elle. Carrying Pix was like carrying a small bag of bricks. The jeep was a quarter of a mile away, and every step was difficult.

Elle kept going, stopped to rest, then picked Pix up and continued again. Finally, Interstate 5 came into view. She all but dragged Pix the remaining distance to the jeep. When she arrived, the others were already there.

"You found her!" Flash exclaimed, rushing to Elle's side. "What happened to her?"

"Don't know," Elle huffed, trying to catch her breath.

"Here, let me help," Jay offered. He picked up Pix's limp body and laid it across the backseat of the jeep. "Wow, she's really out."

Elle grabbed a canteen of water and drank.

"She looks sick," Georgia stated.

Brilliant observation, Elle thought.

"What do you think happened?" Jay asked, studying Pix's face.

"I think she wandered off, got lost and dehydrated, and I don't know what else happened to her," Elle shrugged. "Can we just keep going, please? It's not safe to stay in one place this long."

Georgia was standing to the side, digging through her backpack. She removed a new package of cigarettes. It seemed like they were the only things Georgia had taken the time to salvage from the city.

Elle pulled back Pix's shirtsleeves and searched for open wounds on the girl's body, but there was nothing. It looked like Pix was ill. Her eyelids fluttered open for a moment and she struggled to speak. Instead, she leaned to the side, vomited on the seat, and passed out again.

"Gross," Georgia muttered, frowning.

Elle wrinkled her nose.

"She might have food poisoning," Elle stated. "I've had it before, it's a lot like this."

"Food poisoning from *what*?" Georgia demanded.

"Anything. We're eating supplies scavenged from the city, and not everything is guaranteed safe," Elle pointed out. "When I was first living in the city after Day Zero, I ate something that had gone rotten and I got sick. Almost died."

"How'd you get over it?" Flash asked.

"I found some antibiotics at a pharmacy," Elle replied. "It saved my life."

Elle folded her arms across her chest.

If Pix was going to survive, they were going to have to do *something.*

It would be dangerous.

Chapter Thirteen

2 Days Later

Elle held her breath, crouched behind the pharmacy counter. Jay was right behind her, a bottle of antibiotics in his hand. Elle's heart raced. Early morning sunlight filtered through the dirty windows of the looted pharmacy.

"Where are they?" she breathed.

"They're coming around the back," Jay answered.

Elle closed her eyes and prayed for a way out.

They'd come into town – just the two of them – in a desperate search for antibiotics from the pharmacy. They didn't expect to find any, but Pix was fading fast. She had barely regained consciousness in two days, and her heart rate was slowing down. Elle and Jay had found an old strip mall. The standard buildings were here; former clothing outlets, fast food restaurants and nail salons. Everything was empty, and only about a mile from the freeway, where Georgia and Flash were watching over Pix.

Everything had been fine. The strip mall was abandoned. Elle had entered the front of the pharmacy just as a parade of vehicles rumbled down the boulevard on the street. Vehicles meant trouble. Vehicles meant Omega.

Elle and Jay had run into the building, searching frantically for the antibiotics. They had been fortunate enough to find a limited amount of medicine, but the patrols were checking the buildings. Omega men, dressed in their dark uniforms, were going through each one. What were they searching for? Elle didn't know. She didn't care.

Now they were hiding in the back of the pharmacy, behind rows of empty medical shelving. The patrols were getting closer to their building. There was nowhere to run. A wide, open parking lot in the shopping center made it impossible to escape without being spotted by the patrols. The back entrance was a no-go, too. Patrols were checking the rear entrances.

"We're screwed," Jay whispered.

"We have to hide," Elle replied.

"Where? There's nowhere to go!"

Elle looked around. The pharmacy was huge, but it had been torn apart. Aisle dividers were overturned, trash littered the floor and shattered glass was sprinkled across every surface. The rumbling engines of the trucks outside rattled the walls.

"We can climb into the air vents," Elle said. "Come on!"

She jumped up and rolled over the counter, staying low to the ground. The front of the store was filled with high shelving that was bolted to the wall. She swung herself up, climbing each level until she reached the top. Jay did the same.

Elle pointed to the large air vent in front of them. They were big – about three feet wide and two and a half feet tall. "Come on," she said. "We can fit."

"This is crazy," Jay muttered.

They worked to unscrew the vent from the duct, setting it aside.

"Go first," Elle instructed. "I'll follow."

"But-"

"-Just *do* it!"

Jay crawled inside the vent, making an ungodly amount of noise. Elle watched him disappear into the dark passageway. She crawled in feet first, pulling the vent in behind her. She slowly backed up, farther and farther away from the opening.

They said nothing.

Eventually the door to the pharmacy opened and the patrols came into the store. The voices of the men were clear.

"Find anything here?"

"No one."

"Copy that. There's no sign of militia activity here."

"Well, did you really think we were going to find any sign of them, anyway?"

A pause.

"The National Guard is heading north," someone said, their voice echoing off the walls. "Didn't the Colonel tell you? We captured Commander Young. They're taking him to Los Angeles."

"What about the other one – Cassidy Hart?"

"No idea where she went. I'd like to kill her myself, though. The reward is huge, enough to set me up for life."

"There's a lot of that going around…"

The voices faded into the distance as the patrols left the building. Elle held her breath, the cramped walls of the vent pressing on her hips and shoulders. They waited several minutes before crawling out.

"That was uncomfortable," Jay breathed, pulling himself onto the top of the shelf. "But good thinking, Elle."

Elle nodded.

"Did you hear what they were saying? They were looking for militia groups," she said. "They captured someone important."

"Chris Young," Jay replied. "And Cassidy Hart. They're both pretty well known leaders in the militia groups. We used to hear the militias talk about both of them on the radio in the bunker."

"I've heard of them, too," Elle mused. "Sometimes the Klan would talk about what was going on in the Central Valley. That was how I got information about the outside world."

They sat on the top shelf, lapsing into silence.

"We should get back," Jay said, clearing his throat.

"Yeah." Elle swung her legs over the side and climbed down. They crept to the front of the pharmacy and peeked out the window. The vehicles were gone. The coast was clear.

Elle and Jay shared a glance as they put the antibiotics into Elle's backpack. This was their last shot. If Pix didn't get better, she would die. And they would have to move on without her.

It was a harsh reality.

It was the world that Day Zero had created.

The antibiotics didn't seem to help Pix at first.

"We can't move on until she gets better," Flash said.

"We need to get to Sacramento," Jay replied. "They'll be able to help us. They'll have medical supplies and doctors there, if the rumors are true."

"And if they're not? Pix will die," Flash argued.

Two days had passed since they had administered the antibiotics to Pix. She didn't seem to be recovering. She was comatose, in and out of consciousness. Elle had found a gash in Pix's left hip. It was infected, poisoning the rest of her body. Elle's guess was that Pix had been injured since they had rescued her from the Klan, and the infection from the open wound had finally caught up with her.

"I'm not staying here," Elle said, leaning against the hood of the jeep. "There are Omega patrols in the area, and they could come back. And let's not forget that there could be nomads out here. Bad people."

"Really?" Georgia slammed the door to the jeep, eyes flashing. "We're supposed to be a *team*, Elle. You can't just leave us. That's selfish and irresponsible!"

"It's called self-preservation," Elle replied. "We all need to move forward, no matter *what* is happening to Pix."

"Just give her some more time," Flash pleaded. "We can afford to wait."

"We've been here for four days," Elle pointed out. "That's long enough."

"But anything could happen out there on the road. Pix might get more sick if we try to travel."

"We have a *jeep*," Elle snapped. "We also have *gas*. We can do this."

"Yes, we could do that," Jay answered. "But we can also stay here. We don't need to keep moving if we don't *have* to. We can wait until Pix is better, *then* we can move on. At least until she's conscious."

Elle stared at the sky. Jay was right, of course. They *both* were. They could stay here, relatively safely, and wait for Pix to regain consciousness before they moved on. Or they could keep working their way toward Sacramento. Elle hated the thought of sitting here, waiting. She wanted to be in Sacramento. She was tired of the day-to-day stress of survival. She was tired of arguing with them, tired of pointing out the obvious, only to have them ignore her advice. She wanted to be safe. She was exhausted, traumatized, shocked. She'd been through so much since Day Zero.

Elle didn't want to wait for a happy ending anymore.

She wanted to grab it.

Georgia, Jay and Flash continued to bicker, their voices getting higher and louder. Elle hated the arguing. It was stupid. To stay alive, they needed to pull together.

"There is *no* reason for us to keep moving on," Jay said, turning to Elle, his voice harsh. "When Pix stabilizes, we'll leave."

"But I don't want to *stay here!*" Elle yelled.

"Then *leave!*" Jay snapped.

Elle flinched.

There was a long, tense silence. Georgia swallowed.

At last, Elle said, "Don't be your own worst enemy. Omega might try to kill us, but in the end, you can do a pretty good job of getting *yourself* killed."

Getting killed was easy.

Staying alive...that was the hard part.

Elle left during the night. Jay and Georgia had argued for hours. Flash had withdrawn, and Elle had removed herself from the conversation. They were being stupid and petty. All they had to do was drive, but no one could agree to move forward. There was no majority decision, just factions of disagreement.

I can't believe this, Elle thought.

She had taken her share of supplies and ammunition and disappeared into the night, leaving them behind. She wanted to get to Sacramento. She wanted to do it now, and she couldn't bear to wait any longer. The last year had been hell, and she had no intention of stretching the torture out any longer than she needed to.

She covered mile after mile, stopping to rest when the sun rose. She ate a quick meal, drank some water, and continued. The freeway extended endlessly, but the mountains were beautiful. Elle was exposed on the highway, so she kept a sharp lookout for any unsavory characters. She avoided rest areas and roadside restaurants. It wasn't worth the risk.

She heard something slap against the concrete. She checked her shoelaces. Nothing. She heard it again, and this time she recognized the sound, snapped out of her daze.

Gunshots.

She looked behind her. A small pillar of black smoke was rising into the air in the distance.

She froze, slowly rising to her feet.

The kids, she thought.

The anger was gone, replaced with concern. She started walking back, toward the pillar of smoke. She kept going, jogging. It took several hours to reach the campsite again, and by the time she did, the black smoke had mostly dissipated. She ran forward. The bush that they had been hiding behind was gone, charred to the roots. The jeep was overturned, smoking. The supplies had been grouped into a pile and the remains were smoldering.

"Jay!" Elle cried, dropping her backpack to the ground. "Georgia?"

She rounded the jeep.

Pix was lying on the ground at an unnatural angle, her arm thrown to the side. A ribbon of red blood trailed down the side of her mouth. Elle dropped to her knees and checked Pix's pulse. Nothing. Her skin was cold.

"Pix?" Elle sobbed. "Pix, no. Please..."

Tears streamed down her face. Pix's shirt was stained with blood. She had been shot. Elle hugged the dead girl to her chest and rocked back and forth, weeping. She laid her body in the dirt and crawled to her feet. The world spun around her. She vomited on the gravel, clutching her stomach.

She crawled to the other side of the jeep, away from Pix's body. She stood again and stared at the hood of the jeep. It had been spray painted with gold stars. Georgia, Flash and Jay were nowhere in sight.

The militias couldn't have done this, Elle thought. *They would never kill innocent people. They're meant to defend us from Omega.*

Something had happened.

Elle looked at the freeway. Thick, rubbery tire tracks led away from the scene of destruction. An Omega Humvee was lying on its side, blown apart. A dead Omega soldier was lying on the ground. Elle didn't move, afraid to get near the vehicle.

A militia group must have stopped Omega, Elle deduced.

Omega had clearly found the children. They had succeeded in killing at least two of them, until a militia group – at least that's what Elle assumed they were – stopped them. But where were the other kids?

Taken. The militia must have taken them.

But why?

Elle studied the tracks on the road.

And she started following them.

Epilogue

The old man shoved his flight cap into the pocket of his leather jacket. The wind whipped his gray hair into circles as he climbed out of the seat of an aged biplane. He could taste the salt in the air. The spray of the ocean waves hitting the rocks.

"Manny?"

The old man turned, his face dissolving into a maze of wrinkles.

"Cassidy," he said. "What is it, my girl?"

The woman was small, dressed in combat fatigues. Red hair fluttered against the breeze. "You're not going to believe this," the woman said. "But I think we found your niece."

Manny's hand dropped to his side, limp.

"Elle?" he said.

The woman nodded.

To Be Continued in

Day One

The Second Installment in *The Zero Trilogy*

More Titles by Summer Lane:

The International Bestselling Collapse Series

Book One: State of Emergency

Book Two: State of Chaos

Book Three: State of Rebellion

Book Four: State of Pursuit

Book Five: State of Alliance (COMING JANUARY 2015)

xxx

The Zero Trilogy

Day Zero

Day One: COMING MARCH 2015

End of Day: COMING OCTOBER 2015

xxx

Acknowledgements

Day Zero is different than *The Collapse Series* in that it shows the survival situation of the most average citizens: children. These kids are not militia members, not snipers, not Navy SEALs. They are the average of the average – the nerdy, the troubled and the self-conscious.

After visiting Hollywood and Santa Monica many times, I wondered what one of the most glamorous urban hotspots on earth would look like after the apocalypse. In *Day Zero,* I found my answer.

I would like to thank my best editor and critic, Don Lane, for his help in getting this book into the world. It is always very important to me to remind my readers that these books would not be the quality that they are without his help.

Thanks to my brother, Rocklin, and my mother, Kathy, for their endless support. Thanks to James and Janice White, to Ellen Mansoor Collier and to my grandparents, Pete and Nancy Petinak. Thank you, Scott, for making me laugh. I love you. The blogging world, of course, has been such a huge help in keeping *The Collapse Series* selling in continents around the world, and I am forever grateful for the support of the reading and writing community.

I'm also full of thankfulness to the local community in which I live, who has supported me as a writer since *State of Emergency* released in January 2013. THANK YOU READERS – you are amazing, and I love hearing from you. Your notes and inquiries every week are so much fun to read, and I love talking with you.

Thank you Jesus for blessing me with the life of a writer, and for giving me the inspiration to pen adventure stories. I love working as a writer. I love teaching writing, I love writing about writing, and I love entertaining people through the medium of the written word. Thank you, Lord! It's all from you.

"Peace I leave with you; my peace I give you. Not as the world gives. Do not let your hearts be troubled and do not be afraid." – John 14:27

About Summer Lane

Summer Lane is the author of the national bestselling Collapse Series, which currently includes *State of Emergency, State of Chaos, State of Rebellion* and *State of Pursuit.* The fifth installment, *State of Alliance,* is releasing January 2015. Summer is also the author of the novella adventures of *The Zero Trilogy* and an upcoming survivalist/science fantasy series that will release in 2015. She owns WB Publishing, Writing Belle Magazine, and is an accomplished creative writing teacher and journalist.

Summer lives in the Central Valley of California, where she spends her time writing, teaching, and writing some more. When she is not writing, she enjoys leisurely visits with friends at coffee shops, dates to the movies, hiking in the mountains and strolling on the beach.

Connect with Summer Lane:

Website:

http://summerlaneauthor.com/

Magazine:

http://writingbelle.com/

WB Publishing:

http://writingbellepublishing.com/

Facebook:

State of Emergency – Collapse Series

Twitter: @SummerEllenLane

GoodReads: Summer Lane

TALK TO THE AUTHOR!

Summer LOVES hearing from readers! Email her at:

summerlane101@gmail.com